THE WELL CABIN

Other titles in this Library

" You ran into me," I said, because I had to say something.

CROWN  LIBRARY

THE WELL CABIN

by
JEAN BLATHWAYT

LUTTERWORTH PRESS
LONDON

For
MARKIN

MARTIN

Printed in Great Britain by
Ebenezer Baylis & Son, Ltd., The Trinity Press, Worcester and London

CONTENTS

CHAPTER ONE

AT AUNT JUNE'S

MY name is Jep; Jeffrey Dunne really, but nobody calls me that except Aunt June and I'll tell you about her in a minute.

I shall be eleven next birthday, and with any luck I shall still be with Aunt June then because I think her place is going to be one of the better ones. You see, I haven't got a home of my own—I don't ever remember having one, and it is all in the day's work to go on to a different place every holiday: and a different school too for that matter, and I don't mind telling you that most of them are pretty mouldy.

I was born in Nigeria; that's in Africa in case you don't know, and because the hot climate made me ill I couldn't live out there with my parents, and then when I was only about four they were both killed in a motor accident, so that's why I can't remember ever having a proper home of my own. After my parents' death I was given what's called a Legal Guardian to look after my money and what happens to me and all that sort of thing, but he's been in Canada for years and years, so I don't remember him either, except that his name is Mr. Mackay.

Only yesterday Aunt June and a taxi met me and my trunk at the station, and brought us over the snowy roads to Blue Gates for the Christmas holidays. That's the name of her house, and it has got blue gates too, and the village is called Dingle-wood Marsh which I think is rather nice.

Well, you'd better meet Aunt June now, and any-way I should think it is time for tea. I'd better go in and find out.

"Is that you, Jeffrey? Take your boots off in the porch won't you, and don't bring all that snow into the hall."

That's Aunt June's voice. It's really quite a nice voice, but when she speaks loudly it squeaks, and that's the way she has been speaking ever since I came. When the voice stops I see Aunt June. She is small and terribly thin, and always smiling, but quite silent. It's been like that all day; first a voice, and then Aunt June, but never both of them to-gether.

Well, this is the setting for my story called *The Well Cabin*. That is how things were for me when my life began to be different. It seems ages and ages ago now, and so much has happened since then, but all the same let's go back to that first day at Aunt June's house, and then go on with the story from there.

I pulled off my wellingtons in the porch and walked over the red polished tiles to the kitchen. The house smelt strongly of polish and soap in every room except the sitting-room which always smelt faintly of lavender. The kitchen was small and bright, and my tea was laid out on the table. Aunt June seemed to have had her tea already, but she hovered about in and out of the room, talking when she was out of it, and silent when I could see her.

"I hope you will be able to amuse yourself in here to-night, Jeffrey," she said from the hall, then she popped through the kitchen and into the larder before adding, "I have a committee meeting in the sitting-room at half past six you see, but I shall put out your supper on a tray all ready."

That was all right by me, and I returned her smile when she came in with the milk jug. Her hair reminded me of the silky fluff on the seeds of wild clematis, and it must have been quite pretty before she began to fade.

I wonder if all people fade like Aunt June has when they get old.

After tea I fetched my album of pressed leaves, and the glue and paper and scissors, and the tin with my latest specimens in it. The best was a skeleton holly leaf—just the ghost of a leaf now, but quite perfect all over; it would be hard to press it flat without spoiling it, but I set to work carefully. It did look like being one of the better places, with plenty of peace and quiet, and time to get on with things I wanted to do. But the evening did not turn out quite as peaceful as I had hoped it would, because Aunt June's committee—all old ladies—kept on peeping into the kitchen before the meeting began, and then when it was over and Aunt June came to fetch the tea things to revive them with, I was asked to come in by the fire and talk to them. I went, but I didn't talk much, and they asked such terribly silly questions: why did I want to make a collection of old leaves—was I going to hang up my stocking for Christmas—did I think I was going to like living here? (I said "Yes" to this one.) And then they started talking about me to each other which was much worse. I only listened vaguely, because it made me nearly sick to be called "a blue-eyed boy", but I did catch one of their remarks, which disturbed me a bit. "It's a pity he looks so delicate," one of them said, "because I don't think he will give Miss Henson any trouble otherwise."

Well, I wasn't really delicate, only a bit thin and washy-looking because of Africa, but it did make me wonder if they had been told about my tropical fever. Sometimes I got it, you see, and it put people into a panic for some reason, and then when I was better they would send me off to somewhere else. I think that was one of the chief reasons why I moved about so much.

Aunt June's committee must have made her braver, because she actually spoke at the same time as being there, even if it was only to say, "Bed time, Jeffrey."

I got up to go, and the old ladies let out a chorus of "Good nights". It sounded rather like a flock of suddenly disturbed farmyard geese, and I was quite glad to get away.

It was cold upstairs, so I got into bed as quickly as possible. Aunt June brought me up a stone hot-water bottle wrapped in flannel, and she popped it into my bed without a word. Then when she was safely out in the passage again, the voice came suddenly through the keyhole, "Good night, Jeffrey."

I woke in the morning to a completely new world. All the heavy snow clouds had moved away in the night, and the sky was as clear as crystal with a golden sun up in time for breakfast. By ten o'clock the whole countryside was sparkling.

"Aunt June, I'm going out."

I popped my head round the kitchen door, where she was washing-up, with a check apron strung round her middle. I felt anxious for a moment, because sometimes they made me help, but Aunt June just smiled, and when I was in the porch putting on my boots, her voice called out, "Mind you wrap up warm, Jeffrey."

The greys and whites of yesterday were replaced now by the most lovely brightness wherever you looked. I picked some holly and a rose-hip for my collection, then examined a dry chestnut leaf coated with rime, each little jagged tooth of frost a perfect marvel in itself.

Then suddenly I heard voices, three of them, and each quite distinct from the other.

"Gee-whiz! This is a good hill—just like glass. Bet you we'll pass the sound barrier down here."

"Feet first all the same, in case we meet anything at the bottom."

"Bags sit in the middle in case we crash. It's the softest place!"

I looked up and saw them standing at the top of the hill, but I don't think they had noticed me. The first voice was like a shrill fog-horn, and belonged to the smallest of the three, a boy with the brightest red hair you've ever seen. The second voice was sort of matter-of-fact and seemed to belong to the tall one with dark hair, and the third—a happy sort of voice ending off with a giggle—belonged to the girl. I could only tell she was a girl because of her hair which came below her ears, for they were all three in long trousers and startlingly gay jerseys and gloves.

Well, I got into the ditch as quickly as possible, but it wasn't much use, because, with a sudden whining sound something landed right on top of my hiding place, and I found myself mixed up with masses of arms and legs.

"Francis you ass, you steered the wrong way." It was the tall boy picking himself off me, and then from somewhere underneath my legs the fog-horn's red head popped up and roared out:

"I couldn't help it. There was a colossal bump in the road. Get up, Penny." And he began to tug at my arm. Then suddenly he stopped. "Golly! This isn't Penny."

"I'm here. I missed the ditch somehow," said the voice above us, laughing as she spoke.

"Then who the dickens is this?"

Of course they all three stared at me then.

"You ran into me," I said, because I had to say something.

"I say, I'm frightfully sorry. We didn't see you, honestly we didn't. Wherever were you?" said the tall boy.

"I was in the ditch."

"Oh!"

I looked up, and there they were standing above me in a line on the bank, with pink faces and breath coming out like smoke in the frosty air. I felt rather like a fox at bay with the hounds all round me: not as frightened as a fox must feel, but just about as helpless.

"We've never seen you before, have we?" said the one they called Penny, and come to think of it, her hair was something like the colour of a penny just out of the Mint.

"I've never seen you either," I said, hoping they would soon go.

"Can't you get up? Have we squashed you, or something?" she went on. "Shall we pull you out?"

But I saved them this trouble by getting out of the ditch myself, and shaking a great quantity of powdery snow out of my coat. It seemed an awfully drab sort of garment compared with theirs, and it made me wish more than ever that they would soon go away.

"Who are you anyway?" said the fog-horn, though I knew by then that his real name was Francis.

Well, you may think it queer of me, but I didn't feel like telling. I didn't like Francis's tone of voice, and the other two made me feel awkward somehow; new people sometimes do. So I just turned away and kicked at the snow with the heel of my boot.

"Oh, well, if you won't tell us——" Francis turned away too, not interested any more. "Come on, let's find another hill somewhere else."

Penny just looked at me, and Richard tried to be polite by offering me a slide, but I only shook my head, so they all moved off, trailing away rather quietly I thought, and I wondered if I had been awfully rude to them. But there it was! People can be such an awful nuisance, and it had been a lovely morning till they turned up.

In the afternoon I copied the holly and rose-hip

into my nature book, then drew in a mistle-thrush and a blue-tit and a robin which I had seen in the garden, getting their markings right from one of my bird books. Then I tried to write down something good about the weather, but somehow I couldn't find the right words, and I kept on thinking about those three people instead. It's fun trying to write things down as you've seen them, and I had a feeling that I might be able to write something quite good about Richard and Penny and Francis, but I didn't start then, because I didn't want to mess up my nature book with words about people!

We had tea in the sitting-room that afternoon, but Aunt June was in rather a fussy mood, and I guessed she must have got something on her mind. Then at last she came round to saying it.

"I ought to be going to a dressmaking class to-night, Jeffrey. I really ought to go."

"Go then," I said.

"But what about you, dear? I don't think I ought to leave you alone," she went on, "but I really don't want to miss the class. Oh dear, it's quite difficult to know what I should do."

She seemed to need a bit of help, so I tried to make up her mind for her, and it was a colossal relief when she finally said, "Very well, Jeffrey. I will put your supper ready, and you can lock the door after me to keep out the ghosties!"

Poor Aunt June—if she really believed in ghosts she ought to have thought that they can walk straight through doors!

I didn't lock the door. I went out too, about five minutes after Aunt June so that we wouldn't overlap, and set off towards the village, not sure of my purpose, but in an exploring sort of mood.

I turned up a side way between high stone walls and stopped in front of a door in one of the walls. It looked like a garden door, and suddenly wanting to see what was on the other side, I opened it softly and took a pace inside. Immediately I fell down some steps on to a path. It was hard and stony because someone had swept the snow away, and it hurt my knee a bit, but I was right about it being a garden. Someone had built up a snow castle on the lawn, and put a candle at the top of it so that the light shone over the snow in a circle round it. It was freezing so hard that the tiny bit of warmth from the candle didn't melt the snow near it at all, and for a few moments I stood with my cold hands wrapped round the flame. I could see the dark shape of a house across the lawn, and one of the downstairs windows was uncurtained, letting out a square of orange light over the snow. While I looked, the sound of music came suddenly from that window, so I crept across to have a look; anyone would have, because it was a nice friendly sound, and anyway I'd always been rather good at concealing myself. I had learnt it in the fields and woods, stalking wild animals and birds, and had found it useful too with human beings.

Well, it was just like a picture inside that room; a great log fire burning away and people sitting about and doing things—a lady knitting, a boy playing the piano and another one making something with coloured paper, and a girl sitting on the floor with her sewing. There was a sort of spaniel-cum-retriever dog too, with a silky coat the colour of fried

15

liver asleep on the rug. I saw a Peter Scott goose picture on the wall, and a huge vase of winter leaves and berries standing on a bookcase. I saw it all in a flash, and I knew in the same flash just who those people were. It seemed extraordinary that I should have walked straight into their garden!

Penny looked up and saw me.

"Look! At the window—it's HIM," she exclaimed.

It was just as if someone had broken the whole picture after that. The dog barked, Richard stopped playing, and everyone started up towards the window, thimbles and knitting needles scattering all over the place.

I bolted across the garden, absolutely mad with myself for showing up like that, but I hadn't even reached the gate before a beam of light from a powerful torch picked me out like a searchlight.

CHAPTER TWO

RICHARD, PENNY, AND FRANCIS

"IT is him," bellowed the fog-horn, "the sneaking little burglar! After him, Richard, before he goes off with our toboggan."

Well, obviously I wasn't going to stand for that.

"I'm not taking anyone's toboggan," I shouted back.

"Our bicycles then," Francis yelled.

"I didn't know you had any beastly bicycles."

It wasn't really necessary to shout now, because Francis and I were almost touching noses, and I think we both felt suddenly a bit daft. But Richard had come up too with the torch, and his voice was more friendly, as he said,

"Hello! Did you want something?"

"I was looking at your snow castle."

"Not bad, is it? Why not come inside?"

I couldn't think of a reason why not, especially when the dog bounded out to join us and shoved his warm nose into my cold hands in the most welcoming sort of way.

"All right," I said, and we went back to the house. But Francis was still suspicious of me. It gave me a prickly feeling up the back of my neck, like you feel when you think a bull might be going to turn nasty!

It was very bright and warm inside, and everyone seemed to be in the hall to meet me, Penny and her mother, and another person who hadn't been in the room when I first looked.

"Your knee's bleeding," Penny said at once, and I was glad she said it because it gave us something to talk about.

"I fell down your steps," I said. "You ought to warn people with a notice."

"Yes, I really think we ought to," their mother agreed. "It always takes visitors by surprise."

Francis was looking at me with his head down a bit, like the bull I was talking about.

"What do you want?" he demanded suddenly, and when I didn't answer him, his mother said instead,

"Come in by the fire. You must be frozen," which was a much more sensible thing to say.

"I've guessed you're Miss Henson's relation," Penny said. "Is that right? I've been thinking you out all the afternoon."

"She's a sort of relation," I said. "My only proper Aunt lives in Australia."

"Why?" Francis said aggressively.

"Why not!" Richard put in mildly, adding, "Are you really living at Blue Gates?"

I nodded. We were all sitting down now, and that other person pulled off my wet boots. My feet were frozen stiff, but as soon as the heat got to my toes they began to itch like mad, so that I had to tuck my feet underneath me to get them away from the blaze.

"Chilblains? Bad luck," she said, and I smiled because it was jolly clever of her to have guessed. She looked rather decent, I thought; grown-up, but—well, nice.

18

Then the front door slammed, and everyone sprang up again.

"Daddy—three cheers!" Penny shouted.

He came in, a tallish man with a friendly, tired-looking face. I would have known him anywhere for Richard's father because they were awfully alike.

"Hello!" he said, looking at me, and I thought I saw a twinkle in his eye.

"Hello!" I said.

"He's Miss Henson's relation and he's come to live at Blue Gates because his only proper Aunt lives in Australia," Penny explained in one breath.

"Is that so? Well, welcome to Dinglewood Marsh," he said.

I thought I ought to make some suitable reply, but I didn't know what.

"Haven't you got any other relations?" Penny asked then.

They all ask this question sooner or later, so I can usually get my family history over fairly quickly which is a good thing, because it gets very boring after a time. It made them all a bit quiet like it always does, but Penny came round first and said:

"Why don't you adopt Mummy and Daddy and Henrietta as Aunts and Uncles, then we could all be your cousins by adoption."

"No fear!" Francis said, but everyone else seemed to think it was a good idea, and I suddenly found they had arranged it for me: Aunt Bridget, Uncle Clive, and just "Henrietta" because that was what everyone called her. I discovered that she was Uncle Clive's sister.

He took me off to tie up my knee then, because I

was putting blood on the chair cover, and I guessed he must be a doctor because we went into a room which smelt like a hospital and had rows of bottles on the shelves. He left the door open, and while he was fetching his bag from the car I heard the others talking. I don't think I was really meant to hear, but unless I had my fingers into my ears I simply couldn't have helped it.

"Why can't we have him for Christmas, Mum?" I think it was Richard's voice.

"Oh no! He'd spoil everything." That was Francis all right.

"I don't see why," Penny said.

"I think that's a wonderful idea," Henrietta said, "especially if we invite Miss Henson as well——"

Then Uncle Clive came back and I didn't hear any more.

"What do you think of Dinglewood Marsh?" he asked me, getting to work on my knee.

"It's all right," I said. "A nice name too."

"It means 'A deep little wooded hollow on the boundary'," he went on. "The word 'Marsh' is a corruption of 'March' which means the boundary line between counties."

"Are we on a boundary line?" I asked.

"Yes. Just about. If you go over the fields a bit to a certain wood, you can stand with one foot in this county and the other in the next."

"Have you got a map?" I asked suddenly. It would be fun to find the exact spot and do this.

He went to a cupboard and took one out.

"Like to borrow it? It's a nice big one—three inches to the mile."

"Yes I would, if you wouldn't mind," I said, and put it inside my jersey.

Then we went back to the others, and Francis spotted the bulge at once. I was afraid he might, but it was too big to put in my pocket.

"There you are! He's stolen something already, What did I tell you!" he exclaimed, pointing at my middle.

Everybody said, "Francis!" except Henrietta who just laughed.

"It's a chest-protector I gave him to keep out the cold," Uncle Clive said, and this made Francis mad. He made a dive at me and snatched at the map to see what it really was. But I wasn't having any, and dodged away from him, bumping against the vase on the bookcase. It went over with a frightful crash.

"Well, *now* he's done something awful anyway," Francis bellowed triumphantly, "and that's Mummy's very bestest vase too."

"And whose fault was it, I should like to know," Penny said jumping up from the hearth rug. The dog jumped up too, barking loudly, and I wished that I had never come near the place. There was water and leaves and broken glass all over the floor at my feet.

I don't quite know what happened next, but I was conscious of Richard and Henrietta picking up the bits, and Aunt Bridget fetching a mop, and Penny clutching at the dog and bawling at Francis who bawled back at her. I saw Uncle Clive go out of the room with his hands over his ears, and I didn't blame him. You've never heard such a row.

Well, things quietened down after a bit, and I

would have told Aunt Bridget I was sorry if Francis hadn't been there, because it was really all his fault. The dog came over to me and pushed his nose into my hand, and I bent down to pat him.

"Beaver trusts him anyway," Penny said, "and you've always said he's a jolly good judge of character Francis, so what?"

"So nothing!" Francis said. "Shut up!"

"Can't you two stop arguing?" Aunt Bridget said, collecting her knitting together and getting up. "Find something sensible to do, and entertain your guest properly. I'm going to get the supper."

Francis retired into a corner of the sofa with a book about space ships, and Henrietta sat me down in the best comfortable chair. Penny got going with her sewing again; it was a yellow velvet pin-cushion for her grandmother, she told me, but I thought it looked more like a lump of fungus, and Richard flopped into another chair with a sigh, remarking,

"Peace at last. Glory! What a din. We aren't always quite as bad as this."

"You haven't been here very long, have you?" Henrietta asked me presently.

"Only two days," I said.

"How are you and Miss Henson going to spend Christmas?" Penny asked next, and I remembered the overheard conversation.

"I don't know," I said, "she hasn't said anything."

"We have an absolutely wonderful time," Penny said, adding hurriedly, "and I expect you will too."

She bit off her cotton and held up the lump of fungus for general inspection.

"There, that's finished," she said. "I hope Granny'll like it."

Then she folded her hands on her lap and looked at me seriously.

"D'you know, you haven't even told us your name yet," she said.

"Haven't I? It's Jep," I said.

"Is that all! Mine is Penelope Anne Georgina Sorsbie. Isn't it awful?"

I grinned. It was rather a mouthful, but Penny suited her all right.

"Jeffrey really," I said, "but nobody calls me that except Aunt June."

"How old are you?"

"Nearly eleven."

"Gosh! You don't look it," Francis put in.

"I'm eleven and a month," Penny went on, "and Richard's thirteen. Dear little Francis is only nine, that's why we have to make allowances for him."

"Why not come Christmas shopping with us to-morrow?" Richard said suddenly.

"Would you like to come, Jep?" Henrietta asked me.

"No thank you," I said as politely as I could. There was that map of Uncle Clive's still under my jersey, and I had made other plans for the day.

"Have you finished all your shopping, then?" Penny asked.

"I don't usually do any," I said.

"Haven't you got any money?" Francis couldn't keep out of the conversation, and this possibility seemed to interest him.

"Yes, I've got some," I said, "I get one-and-six a week pocket money."

"Then why don't you buy presents for other people?" Francis went on. "I call it jolly mean."

Well, I wasn't going to tell him that I saved it up to buy bird books, although it did suddenly strike me that perhaps I ought to get a new vase for Aunt Bridget. I managed to get Henrietta alone later on and asked her how much it would cost.

"You could get a very good one for five shillings," she said.

I thought for a minute, and then said, "D'you think you could get one for me—if I give you the money?"

"I'll pay half, if you like," she said, which was jolly decent of her, because it really ought to have been Francis.

I stayed to supper, then Uncle Clive drove me home in the car. Aunt June arrived back from her class at the same time, and there was a bit of a commotion for the first few minutes.

"Oh! Dr. Sorsbie—whatever is Jeffrey doing in your car? Is he all right?"

"Perfectly all right, Miss Henson. He invited himself to supper with us."

"Dear me, what an extraordinary thing to do. I do believe I ought to have stayed at home after all."

"Nonsense!" Uncle Clive said, giving me a wink. "We've had a very happy evening. Whenever you have to be out, Miss Henson, just send him around to us."

CHAPTER THREE

THE MAN WITH SNOWSHOES

THE air was crisp and frosty still in the morning, the sun giving a warm smell to the countryside without thawing it anywhere. I cut a stout ash stick out of the hedge to use as a staff, and set off up the lane behind Blue Gates, prodding the ground in front of me as I walked in case the drifts should be deep. I wasn't a bit sorry that I hadn't gone out with the Sorsbies, although I did hope that I might be able to meet them again some time. Nothing more had been said about Christmas.

I crossed a field and paused at the next gate, looking cautiously over it and listening intently. Another white field stretched away in front of me, then the ground rose gently upwards, and over the brow of the little hill I could see what looked like the beginnings of a wood. I spread out the map on the snow, and guessed that it must be the wood Uncle Clive had meant. Nothing living was in sight, and except for the tapping of a bird's beak on a tree there was no sound either. I followed up the tapping, keeping near to the hedge and not hurrying because the frozen snow crunched under my boots, and in the great silence the sound was magnified a hundred times. Suddenly the tapping stopped, and I heard a few short twittering notes like the sound a pebble makes when you bounce it across ice. I knew that note, and gazing upwards into an elm tree saw a small greyish-blue bird with orange breast feathers creeping along its branches: a nuthatch—I had often watched one before. It disappeared round the other side of the trunk, popped out again higher up, then the tapping began once more. I hoped it would succeed in finding lots of juicy insects in the crevices of the elm bark.

I worked out from the map where the boundaries met, then went through the gate into the wood. There were lots of little animal tracks in the snow now, rabbits mostly, and quite a few birds, then nearer to the hedge the neat footpads of a fox. Foxes are such awfully secret creatures: they make use of every little bit of cover they can find. I followed up a moorhen's tracks to a small pond, but there were no birds about and the water was bound up with ice, so they must have gone off somewhere else in search of unfrozen streams. Then I found a path round the edge of the wood.

I hadn't gone far before a great brown bird skimmed suddenly in from the fields, turned sharply through a gap in the hedge and swooped down on to something. It was some wretched small bird, for I heard a little screech of pain as the sparrow-hawk's talons gripped it. But I couldn't help admiring the big bird as I watched it winging its way back across the fields with its dashing onward flight. And after all, it's the old law of tooth and claw, and it's no good feeling sorry for the prey; it's just the way Nature works.

I think I found the boundary line all right. It was

right in the corner of the wood—according to the map, so I stood for a moment with each leg in a different county. Quite a superior feeling! Then I went on up the track to the gate at the other end of the wood. Here I found some marks in the snow which puzzled me a lot; indistinct, shuffling marks, each about a yard and a half long, but not very deep in the snow, and rather like a tennis racket in shape. I followed them up a short lane and through another gate, and found myself face to face with a small stone cottage. Of course I bobbed down behind a bramble bush at once, but as nothing happened I had another look.

It seemed a nice sort of place, with friendly windows and a little porch going up over the door into a point. The garden was just a wilderness surrounded by a broken-down fence, and a rusty iron pump without a handle stood up dark against the snow. The place seemed quite deserted. Then I smelt something; strong, rather unusual tobacco smoke drifting down to me on the still air from the cottage. I crept up and hid myself inside a small shrubbery of evergreens near one of the downstairs windows. A pane of glass was missing, and the smell was much stronger now, and I could hear a faint scratching sound as well. Raising myself cautiously I put one eye to the corner of the window. At first it looked all dark in contrast to the whiteness outside, but after a bit, as I got used to it, I began to make out the room.

Yes, there was somebody there all right, sitting in the chimney-corner, with a pad of paper on his knee and writing away like mad; that was the scratchy sound I had heard. A pipe was sticking out of his mouth; that's where the smell was coming from, but it was his clothes which fascinated me most. I had never seen anything quite like them before. The jacket was made of leather, with fur round the collar, and a sort of leather fringe below the shoulders all the way round. His trousers were like riding breeches, and his boots came up to his knees. A hat with a big brim lay on the floor beside his pack, and propped up against one of the walls was a pair of snowshoes. These, I supposed, accounted for the odd tracks I had found in the snow.

Well, I watched him for a long time, and he just went on writing and writing without stopping once, so in the end I went back to the wood, and then home to dinner. But of course I was going to come back.

Aunt June was getting quite brave now and talking to me, and it certainly made things easier. During dinner she said,

"I have made a little plan for you, Jeffrey. I have to go out again this evening, so I have asked dear Mrs. Sorsbie if some of her nice family can come along and keep you company."

"Oh!" I said. It was kind of Aunt June, but I had really wanted to get on with my nature book. All the same I managed to get quite a lot done before Penny and Henrietta turned up soon after tea.

"Richard's busy, so he couldn't come," Penny said, "I think it's to do with his Christmas surprise. Francis won't come. What have you been doing all day?"

"I went out," I said, "and I think I found the boundary."

"What boundary?"

"Between this county and the next. Uncle Clive lent me his map. It goes right across the corner of the wood, and I stood in two counties at the same time."

Penny laughed. "What did it feel like?"

"All right," I said, and then I added—almost before I had decided whether to or not, "and I found something else as well."

"What?"

"A man."

"What sort of a man?"

"Oh! a good one. Like—like a Red Indian a bit."

"A Red Indian?" Penny sounded amazed. "Had he got feathers on his head?"

"Oh no," I said, and I couldn't help laughing. "Just ordinary hair."

"What made you think he looked like an Indian, Jep?" Henrietta asked.

"I—I don't really know, unless it was his coat. It had a sort of fringe all round the shoulders—oh, and he had snowshoes too."

Of course they wanted to know where I had found him, so I told them about the cottage.

"That's the old keeper's cottage," Henrietta said. "Nobody's lived there for years. I think the well ran dry."

"Well, somebody's living there now," I said, "at least, he's staying there anyway."

"Tell me about him," Penny said.

"I've told you."

"Is that *all* you know?"

29

"Yes, I didn't want to disturb him. But I'm going back to-morrow."

"Oh can I come, please? And all the others?"

Well, I wasn't sure. I wouldn't mind Penny and Richard—not really, but Francis might be a problem.

Then Henrietta said, "Don't worry about Francis. He'll behave all right," just as if she had read my thoughts.

So we arranged to meet at the top of the lane behind Blue Gates at about ten o'clock in the morning.

They turned up in good time, Beaver too, but I couldn't help feeling a bit fed up with what they were wearing.

"Anything wrong?" Richard asked, looking at my glum face.

"Those clothes," I said, pointing to their red and blue and yellow jerseys. "They show up like signals against the snow, and we want to scout a bit."

"Gosh! Yes," Richard said. "You mean disguise ourselves? We ought to have thought of that. Shall we go back and change?"

"I'm not going back for anyone," Francis said.

"Then you shan't come with us!" Penny put in.

"Oh, shut up!" Richard said mildly. "We're just wasting time. Come on, Francis." And he took hold of his brother by the sleeve of his yellow jersey.

"I'll take Beaver," I said, putting my hand on his collar, "and we'll wait for you at the bottom gate into the wood."

I had to wait quite a time for them, but at last they turned up looking much more ready for stalking.

Penny was in a dun-coloured mackintosh, and Richard and Francis had sort of overalls over their other clothes and light-coloured windcheaters on top.

"Our space-suits!" Francis said brightly.

We divided into two parties then so that we could take different paths through the wood, and look out for footprints and clues. Penny and Beaver came with me, and the boys went off together. Penny was quite a good stalker, and Beaver kept to heel all the time, and we only had one really anxious moment when a wood pigeon clattered suddenly out of the branches above us.

"Sorry," Penny whispered, because she had just put the whole of her weight on to a dry stick, and of course it had gone off like a pistol shot.

We didn't find any interesting clues, but Richard had picked up a plug of burnt-out tobacco. He held it out in the palm of his hand, and I sniffed at it suspiciously. Yes, it belonged to our man all right.

"But you know, Jep, he can't have got any feet!" Richard said with a laugh. "I swear we didn't see a single human footprint."

"P'rhaps he flies," Francis said. "He's probably just arrived from the moon. Golly! D'you think he has—p'rhaps he came on a flying saucer?"

"He wears snowshoes," I said, "and they don't leave much mark."

"Honestly?" Richard said.

"Yes. I saw them through the window."

"Why d'you think he wears them?" Richard wondered. "The snow isn't all that deep."

"He probably doesn't want to be tracked down,"

31

I said, "I mean, nobody would recognize the tracks of snowshoes. I didn't."

"Neither did we," Richard put in. "This sounds rather exciting. I wonder what sort of a person he is?"

"We'll soon find out," I said.

We went through the gate, and stalked up to the cottage over the snow. I could see that Richard knew the proper way, wriggling forward on his front and using his elbows and toes to move by, but Penny and Francis humped along with their tails high in the air.

"Tails *down*!" Richard hissed. "You look like a couple of camels."

"I feel like one," Penny giggled, collapsing on to the snow.

"Make use of the bushes, and the bumps in the ground," I whispered. "Watch Richard."

He was forging ahead of us like a proper commando, and soon we had all arrived safely in the shrubbery, and were able to sit up for a breather.

"It needs practice," Penny said in a loud whisper. "D'you think he saw us?"

"Shouldn't think so," I said, sniffing hopefully for that tobacco smell. The place felt awfully deserted somehow, and I couldn't smell a thing except the peppermint in Francis's mouth.

"We'd better try the windows," I whispered. "Last time he was in there." And I got up cautiously to look. But as I had feared the room was quite empty. Richard skulked off round the cottage to look in the other windows, but there didn't seem to be anyone about. They suggested I should go inside after that, and as the door was unlocked I went in, and up the stairs into all the funny little rooms, but they were all quite empty. So I went down again and let in the others.

"No luck, I'm afraid," I told them. "We'd better search around in here for a clue. This was the room he was using."

But we couldn't find anything helpful anywhere, only some burnt-out wood-ash in the hearth which seemed horribly conclusive somehow.

"Looks as if he'd hopped it," Richard remarked.

"Yes," Penny said, very crestfallen.

"It's all a trick!" Francis declared, "I bet you Jep invented the whole thing."

Well, I wasn't going to argue with Francis but I admit I did feel a bit disappointed.

CHAPTER FOUR

A MESSAGE FROM THE FUGITIVE

WE had all rather given up looking for clues, except Penny who was still poking hopefully about round the fireplace, when she suddenly gave a shout of excitement.

"Look! There's a loose brick here. It comes right out, and there's a hole inside full of papers."

We gathered round her as she pulled out great wads of folded paper, all of it written on in small close handwriting. Then at the very back of the hole—and her arm went in almost up to the shoulder, she found an oilskin tobacco pouch, two boxes of matches, a packet of tea, a tin of milk and an electric torch.

"I say, what a store!" Richard said.

"An escaped prisoner," Francis shouted. "Let's hide all his stuff for a lark."

I would have punched his head for that remark if there hadn't been more important things to do.

"Supposing he is?" Penny said nervously, "and he comes back and finds us?"

"No, I'm sure he's not that," I said, "he's more likely a sort of fugitive come here to get away from people—to get on with his writing."

"That's it—an author!" Richard cried triumphantly. "I bet you he is. Come on, let's have a look at those papers." He took them from Penny, and unfolded one of the wads. "Listen to this," he said, and then he began to read:

"The temperature had been falling fast all the afternoon, and was just touching 45° below zero when we tied up the dogs for the night. Unharnessing tired sledge dogs, and carrying provisions after a long day's travelling across ice-bound lakes, can be the last straw to a cold and weary man, but when the fire gets roaring away in the stove and the candles are lit on the shelves, you can look out again at the stars above the pine trees with a great peace and thankfulness in your heart."

Richard reads awfully well, and we were all a bit silent for a minute. Then he said, "Not bad! I reckon he *is* an author, Jep."

"Yes," I said, longing to ask him to read more, but somehow it didn't seem fair to be prying like this.

"Shall we put it all back?" I said. "I mean—well, it seems a bit unfair, doesn't it?"

"Yes, I agree," Richard said, but I could see that he was longing to go on reading those papers. "He sounds an interesting bloke; sledge dogs, and 45° below zero—that's terrific."

"And snowshoes!" I said suddenly.

"Hmm. Yes," Francis added thoughtfully. "There might be snow on the moon, mightn't there, *and* iced lakes and things——"

"Perhaps he's an explorer," Penny suggested. "He may have been to the South Pole or something."

"Or the North," Francis put in. "That's nearest the moon."

"I'd like to know," Richard said slowly, and we watched him fold up the papers again and then put everything back in the hole. "D'you think we could come back again to-morrow?"

"No good," Penny said. "Dentist in the morning, then tea with the Vicar."

"The next day then?" Richard suggested.

"That's Christmas Eve. Would we have time?" Penny wondered.

"Probably not," Richard said with a frown. "He's probably gone away for Christmas anyhow, and will be coming back afterwards. What about Boxing Day?"

So they agreed to come back on Boxing Day, while all the time I was making quite another plan in my mind.

"We'd better go back," Penny said. "Come on."

They wandered to the door, but I stayed put in the chimney-corner.

"Aren't you coming?" Penny said.

"In a minute. I'll catch you up."

Fortunately they didn't ask any questions, so I was able to write the note in peace, and I made it as short as possible.

Dear Fugitive, I found you yesterday by mistake but you were busy and I didn't disturb you. I'd like to meet you, so if I can will you leave a sign somewhere. I shall be coming back this afternoon by the gate at the bottom of the wood.

Sucking my pencil I wondered how to sign it, and eventually scribbled "From a Friend". Then I tore the sheet out of my notebook, removed the brick

36

again, and with a bumping heart slipped my note inside.

It suddenly seemed so awfully important to me that I should meet this stranger.

I caught up the others in the lane, and Francis looked at me suspiciously.

"Stealing some of his stores I suppose," he said.

"Oh yes of course," I said. "The tobacco's for Aunt June. She smokes a pipe!"

At Blue Gates, Aunt June was busy with things in jars which smelt nice, so it was easy for me to slip off again after dinner.

Our footmarks of the morning were clear in the snow, and I wondered what the fugitive would think of our intrusion. In fact I wondered a lot of things as I tramped over the fields; would he have had time to give me a sign yet—would he want to see me —had he gone away for a long time—what sort of a man was he? In fact I was so busy wondering and doubting and hoping that I almost fell over a branch of a tree lying on the path just inside the wood.

"That's odd!" I thought. "It wasn't here this morning, and there hasn't been any wind all day to blow it down."

It was a branch of ash wood, about as big as me, and more or less dead. The twigs snapped off quite easily. I looked round me, searching for an ash tree which it could have fallen off, but they all seemed to be oaks and beeches just there. Then it suddenly dawned on me that perhaps this was the sign I was looking for. But did it mean yes, or no? I thought hard for a minute, and then decided to go on and look for an ash tree. I found one quite soon, and there was the scar high up on its trunk where the branch had fallen off. The wood looked quite rotten, so it wasn't very surprising. Well! What now? I stood with my hands on my hips looking up at the years of thick ivy-growth curling and entwining itself round the trunk. My eyes went up as far as that scar, almost black with rot in the centre and then suddenly I saw something else. A glint of sunlight between the branches shone on to something bright, something metal. It looked like a small sheath-knife stuck into that bit of rotten wood.

I scrambled up the ivy jolly quickly, and catching hold of the little black handle pulled out the blade, and as I did so a piece of paper fluttered down to the ground: a message! I got down again even quicker, the knife in my hand, and with my heart pounding away at a terrific rate picked up the paper to read it. This is what it said:

> Dear Friend. You must have missed me this morning by just ten minutes, but if you find this note I guess you deserve a welcome. What about after Christmas on St. Stephen's Day at 2 o'clock? Come alone, and give a curlew's whistle from the garden gate, and wait for my answer. You can keep the little knife.

I hadn't a clue when St. Stephen's Day was, but felt sure that Henrietta would tell me without asking any awkward questions.

Well, there wasn't much I could do then, so I wandered back to Blue Gates, and put the knife in the old suitcase where I kept all my other treasures.

The first moments of terrific excitement wore off after a time when I realized I had got to wait now until after Christmas.

Aunt June called me into the sitting-room to "come and have a look".

"All my Christmas cards, Jeffrey. Quite a show isn't it? So many kind people, and so good of them to remember me every year."

I looked at her collection on the mantelpiece, the robins, and the snow scenes, and the holy ones with Mary and Joseph and the Baby, and the shepherds and the kings, but I didn't say anything. I just went outside again and kicked the snow about, and began to think of other Christmases I had spent. Some of them had been quite fun, and some rather boring, and some a bit terrifying because of the tons of strange people about, but on the whole I had always been glad when it was over. I didn't hardly ever feel lonely, but somehow having to have Christmas in other people's families reminded me that I hadn't got a mother of my own, or a proper home either.

After a bit I noticed that Aunt June was watching me from the sitting-room window, so I stopped kicking the snow about and went down to the village. I met Penny coming out of the shop.

"I've just bought some soap for Miss Henson," she said, "because you're both coming to us for Christmas, and I must have a present for her."

"Are we?" I said, suddenly feeling brighter. "Aunt June hasn't said anything yet."

"She will," Penny said, "Mummy's going to see her to-day. Are you glad?"

I grinned at her. "What do you think?" then I

added, "I say, do you think I could give her some soap too? I haven't got her anything yet."

"Yes, I should think so, only don't get pink. Mine's pink!"

So I went in and bought a piece of green soap. It was the biggest piece in the shop, and smelt rather odd I thought. After that I wandered about for more or less the rest of the day wondering how I could ever wait until after Christmas before I went to meet my Fugitive.

CHAPTER FIVE

CHRISTMAS

AUNT JUNE was in a bit of a fuss about leaving Blue Gates empty for two nights, but I knew she was awfully bucked as well about being invited for Christmas.

"So kind of them to want an old woman like me," she kept on saying.

I felt a bit worried, because I knew she had a little parcel for everyone, and I only had one for her, and Aunt Bridget's vase if Henrietta had remembered. I wondered if I ought to have done something about it.

The moment we arrived we were plunged straight into an absolute turmoil of activity. Every room was lit up, and every door was wide open, and people seemed to be running about all over the house. Aunt Bridget appeared out of the muddle with flour on her hands.

"You've just arrived at the crucial moment," she said. "Everything's going up."

"Going up in smoke, if you ask me!" Richard said. "Have you seen the Yule Log, Mum? It's simply colossal."

"Hello, Jep!" Penny called out from the top of a cupboard in the hall, and Francis, sitting astride a step ladder with his arms full of paper chains, looked down at me and said, "Oh—you've come. Then you might as well help with these." He threw down the end of one of the chains. "Hang on, and don't pull or they'll bust. Here Penny, catch this end."

"I want a drawing-pin," Penny called out to the world in general. "Look out, Francis—you're pulling it—there! now it's bust."

"It was you," Francis shouted. "I wasn't even touching it. I *told* you not to pull."

"I didn't!"

"Shut up, you two," Richard said, coming into the hall and standing in the middle with his hands on his hips. "Somebody'd better organize this, or you'll never get the things hanging symmetrically. Drawing-pins coming up, Penny." He threw her a little box which she missed, and drawing-pins showered all over the hall.

"Butter-fingers," Uncle Clive said, striding out of the surgery. "Hello, Jep! Did you ever see such a mess?"

Well, we got them up at last, and the result was rather good. Then the holly and ivy came in in a big sheet, and every picture and shelf had to have its pieces.

You've never seen anything like the Christmas cards they had in the sitting-room; there must have been at least a hundred. Penny found me staring at them.

"After all there *are* six of us," she said, "but Daddy gets the most always because he's such a popular doctor. I got fifteen this year. How many did you get?"

"None," I said.

"Oh, Jep! What a shame."

"It's all right," I said quickly. "Nobody ever knows my address. It's always changing, you see."

Tea was a bit of a scramble because everyone seemed too busy to settle down properly. Uncle Clive had gone out again, and Richard just took a bun and disappeared upstairs.

"He's got a terrific secret," Penny told me, "and nobody knows what it is. It's sure to be awfully good."

After tea Henrietta hung up the mistletoe bough from the middle of the sitting-room ceiling. She had made it all herself, and it was like a great green globe, every section wound round with evergreens, and six rosy apples hanging down in the middle on red ribbons.

"I polished those," Francis said. "It took about a gallon of spit!"

At the very bottom of the globe was the big bunch of mistletoe tied on with a green ribbon, and Uncle Clive came in just when it was fixed.

"Mistletoe," he said at once. "Bags I the first kiss."

"Where's Mummy?" everybody shouted, and somebody fetched her from the kitchen, flour on her hands again.

"What is it? I shall never get those mince pies made," she said, laughing.

"Daddy wants the first kiss. Go on, you must!" And they pushed them underneath the mistletoe bough.

I saw Aunt June wiping her eyes—she's awfully

soft sometimes, but I suppose she can't help it. Then Penny tried to kiss Francis and they had a fight with cushions which only came to an end when Uncle Clive called out,

"All hands to the Yule Log!"

It was nearly as big as me, and it took all of us to carry it into the house.

"Are you going to burn it all at once?" I couldn't help asking.

"Yes. We put it on last thing to-night," Uncle Clive said. "It's good seasoned oak and will burn steadily all through Christmas Day and leave piles of glowing embers."

Everybody began to go off into corners after that, and there was a lot of rustling of paper, and Penny and Francis kept on shouting to each other not to look. I felt a bit lost, and just wandered about until Henrietta appeared and said:

"I've got one or two extras, Jep, if you'd like to come up and have a look?"

Her room was all green and yellow like a primrose wood, and she emptied a basket of things on to her patchwork quilt.

"I've got the vase," she said, taking it out of a drawer. "Will it do, do you think?"

"Thanks awfully," I said. It was a lovely dark green glass one, very like the one I had broken.

Then we went back to the things on the bed.

"I usually have a last-minute shop for emergencies," she said. "How much can you spend?"

"I've got seven and sixpence, after I've paid for the vase. Can I get enough for everyone with that?"

Henrietta thought I could, easily, and we had quite fun choosing from her little store. In the end I chose a Penguin book for Richard, three hankies in a box for Penny, an enormous pencil for Francis, and a pot of glue for Uncle Clive. She gave me coloured paper and string and labels to write on, then I went to my room to tie them all up.

But I still hadn't got anything for Henrietta. My box of treasures was under the bed—I always take it everywhere with me—and I took it out now and laid everything on the eiderdown in lines; a fossil, two cowrie shells, my nature books, the Fugitive's knife, my torch and paint-box, and the new camel-hair brush, and the little ivory box; then there was my pencil-box and bird books, and the skull of a field mouse, and the pheasant's tail feather, and the little log cabin my Guardian had sent me from Canada. It was the only present he had ever sent me, and it was almost my greatest treasure because I had long ago made up my mind to live in a log cabin when I was grown up.

Well, it took me a long time to decide what I should part with, and some of the things wouldn't have been any use to Henrietta anyhow, but in the end I wrapped up the little ivory box because it had never been much use to me. It was too small to hold my specimens, and too bulky outside to get into the pocket of my shorts.

The rest of the evening was a bit of a riot, but Aunt Bridget managed to get us all up to bed by about eight o'clock.

"All fixed for to-morrow?" Richard asked, coming into my room in his dressing-gown. "I've got a few extra things if you happen to be stuck or anything."

"I'm all right," I said. "I've got something for everyone now." But all the same it was decent of him to ask.

"The grown-ups go to the midnight service," he said, "so don't be surprised if you get woken up in the night. At about one o'clock," he added, and I thought he looked a bit sheepish as he said that.

Then they all came in to say "good night", and to make sure I was quite comfortable. Henrietta was the last, and she had a limp looking sock hanging over her arm.

"You might as well have one too," she said. "I'm afraid we haven't grown out of it yet."

I watched her tying it on to the end of my bed.

"There! You might find it full in the morning with any luck."

Then she came and sat on my bed and asked me where I had spent last Christmas.

"In London, worse luck!" I said. "I go somewhere different almost every year."

"A nomad, in fact," Henrietta said. "Like your friend in the keeper's cottage."

"Yes," I said. Then I asked her about St. Stephen's Day.

"It's the same as Boxing Day," she said, and, as I had thought, she didn't ask any awkward questions about why I wanted to know.

Henrietta's like that; she seems to know when you don't want to talk about something. But we did go on talking a bit, and I found myself telling her things I don't tell most people: about all the dull

46

places I'd been to, and the silly people I'd had to stay with, and how I hated towns. Then I told her about my nature books, and she asked if she could see them, so I got out my case and showed them to her.

Henrietta's absolutely the first person who ever saw my nature books.

She seemed interested too, especially in the paintings I had done of birds.

"Did you copy these birds, Jep?" she asked me.

"Only to get the markings right," I said. "I make up the picture from how I remember it looked when I saw it."

"Yes, that's the best way," she said. "To look at real things, and then paint them out of your head. At least, I think it's the best way."

"So do I," I agreed.

Then she told me it was high time I went to sleep, and I did feel a bit dopey because it had been a hectic sort of evening, but after she had tucked me in and gone away I felt awfully happy—sort of safe, as if I really belonged somewhere.

I woke up with a jerk. It was pitch dark except for the stars which were brighter and clearer than I had ever seen them before. The clock downstairs chimed the hour and struck one, and I suddenly remembered what Richard had said. I lay very still listening. There wasn't a sound anywhere, and yet something had woken me up. Then I heard them coming back from the midnight service, the light from their lantern flickering across the ceiling as they passed underneath my window. I heard them come into the hall very quietly and close the door again, then soft footsteps on the stairs.

It was exactly at that moment that the singing began; it sounded like hundreds of voices far away, and yet it seemed to be coming from the landing just outside my bedroom. I got out of bed and peered through the door. Penny and Francis were peering through theirs too, still half asleep, and in the dim half-light I could see the others at the top of the stairs looking too. But I couldn't see Richard anywhere. The singing got louder and louder and then faded out, and another light came on from the corner of the landing where the stairs go up to the attic. It was shining inside a little stable, and there were the figures of Joseph and Mary, and the shepherds, and a donkey and an old cow, all looking down at the little Lord Jesus asleep in the manger. It was jolly impressive, and we all gathered round to see better. Richard had made it awfully well, and he had put his gramophone up the attic stairs for the sound of angels singing.

"I thought it really *was* angels," Penny said, rubbing her eyes. "Oh, isn't Christmas lovely!"

"And a happy Christmas to all of you," Uncle Clive said, and then everyone began to say it too to everyone else. It was rather exciting there in the dim light from the little Crib, and except for being a bit cold, none of us wanted to go back to bed again.

"But I think it will be a happier Christmas still if we can all have a little sleep first," Aunt Bridget said, then she put her arm round Richard's shoulder and

48

added, "It was a lovely surprise, darling, the loveliest you could have thought of."

And we all agreed.

Christmas Day was wonderful, every minute of it. We all went to church in the morning, then stuffed ourselves with turkey and plum pudding, and after everyone had helped with the mountain of washing-up, Henrietta lit the candles on the mistletoe bough and we all piled up our presents for everyone underneath it. Then we had a terrific unwrapping, and hundreds of "thank-yous" went round. Aunt Bridget actually kissed me when she had unwrapped the vase, and Francis said, "Blimey! Jep—it ought to have been me really."

Penny laughed like anything when she discovered that the soap I had bought for Aunt June was only a piece of washing-soap—but how was I to know, and anyway Aunt June seemed jolly pleased, and said it was her "most original present!"

We listened to the Queen at three o'clock, and then went out for a bit of fresh air and exercise. All the same, nobody could eat much tea because of dinner; but we had the crackers and things, and played games, and after supper sang every carol we could think of till everyone had sort of subsided with exhaustion, and all through the whole day the huge oak log glowed slowly away in the grate, the flames charring its surface into a pattern just like the breast feathers of a sparrow hawk.

Nobody wanted to go to bed after such a lovely day, but we had quite fun when we did go up, and Francis and I had a sponge fight in the bath; every-thing got awfully wet, but we helped Henrietta to mop it up, and then when things had properly calmed down she played a lovely quiet record on Richard's gramophone called "Sheep may safely graze", and we lay in bed and listened with our doors open until we felt like going to sleep.

CHAPTER SIX

THE CURLEW'S WHISTLE

I HAD to be a bit beastly to the others the next morning, which was rather unfair after they had been so decent to me, but how else could I have got away alone?

"I've got a beastly headache," I said, sitting on my bed and looking as if I had. "Can't we put off going to the cottage till to-morrow?"

"I'm going to-day, anyway," Francis said.

"I think we ought to wait if Jep's really feeling rotten," Richard said. "After all, it was his discovery."

I gave Richard a sickly sort of smile and said, "Thanks awfully. Sorry to be so dim." Then I put my head in my hands and added that I got these attacks sometimes.

I must have put it on quite well, because Francis stopped arguing, and Penny said, "Bad luck", so sympathetically that I felt meaner than ever.

"Why not ask Daddy for an aspirin?" she said. But I thought this might be taking it too far, and I made them promise not to tell the grown-ups.

"Aunt June would go off the deep end if she knew," I said, "and anyway, I shall be all right to-morrow. I'll come round after breakfast."

We went back to Blue Gates during the morning, and immediately after dinner I slipped away. The weather had changed suddenly to misty dampness, great lumps of snow kept flopping off the big branches. One flopped right on to my head, and the water trickled down my neck, but it only made me laugh out loud because I felt so awfully happy. I was practising the whistle of a curlew in my head, so that I could give a really good one when I got to the garden gate.

Well, I got there, and I whistled, and it *was* a really good one. Anybody might have thought it was a real curlew if they hadn't known that this wasn't curlew country. The Fugitive must have known, and that's why he chose it so that we wouldn't get muddled up with other birds. I waited, and then from behind me in the fields I heard the answer. I turned away from the cottage and looked through a gap in the hedge. Yes, a very tall man was coming over the sodden snow towards me, wearing the same odd clothes, and smoking the same strong tobacco. I scrambled through the hedge and went to meet him, my heart pounding against my ribs like a sledge-hammer.

"Hello!" I said, "I've come."

"Well done! I had a feeling you might," he said, and his voice was very deep and just a bit foreign sounding—American perhaps, I thought.

We came up to each other, and he took my hand in an iron grip which jolly well squashed my fingers.

"How d'you do, my friend," he said, looking into my face.

"How d'you do," I said too. "I found your letter all right. It wasn't awfully difficult."

He smiled then, his teeth showing very white in a rather weather-beaten face.

"Good. Come along inside. I've got some tea brewing."

We went in together, and the cottage felt so familiar that I might have been living there all my life.

"Did you go away for Christmas?" I asked, watching him take a can of boiling water off the fire.

"Yes. I've got a mother, you see. She wanted me to go and stay."

"I haven't got a mother," I said. I thought he ought to know that fairly soon, and I expected him to look at me curiously like they all do, but instead he just poured out the tea into two tin mugs and asked me what my name was.

"It's Jep," I said, because I never could be bothered with all the rest of it.

He did look up at me then, and his eyes seemed to go right through me and out again the other side! I thought he looked rather taken aback for a moment, and I wondered what was so odd about my name.

"I guess you don't remember me," he said, and now it was my turn to look surprised.

I didn't know what to say, and he just laughed and handed me one of the mugs. "After all, you were only a little nipper then. It was years and years ago."

"I'm afraid I don't remember," I said. "I've never seen you before the other day, I'm sure I haven't."

"O.K. Jep." He put some sugar into my tea and stirred it round with his spoon. "My name's Fin, by the way. We both go in for little ones, don't we!"

"I'll tell you my full name if *you'll* tell me yours,"

I said, still staring at him and trying, without any success, to remember.

"I know yours already," he said, "and I'll give you the whole afternoon to guess mine in, if you like!"

"What *is* my name?" I said uncertainly.

He laughed, and sat down in the chimney-corner. "I see you don't believe me, Master Jeffrey Dunne!"

"Then—you do know me?" I gasped.

"Yes, I know you, and I ought to know you a great deal better, my boy. But it's never too late to start. Ever heard of Finlay Mackay?"

"Mr. Mackay—my—my Guardian? Is that *you*?" And as I spoke, of course I realized it all: the clothes, and the snowshoes, and the accent, and that bit of writing about sledge-dogs and frozen lakes; it all added up to a man who had lived in Canada.

"When did you come back, Mr. Mackay?"

"Just two weeks before Christmas," he said. "And my name's Fin, by the way, not Mr. Mackay."

"Had you come to look for me?"

"Yes, I was going to. But I hadn't checked up on where you were living now, and honestly Jep, I didn't know you were down here. If this wasn't the hand of fate just leading us together, then I don't know what fate is!"

"Well, anyway it's a jolly good thing," I said with a sudden tremendous feeling of well-being. "Francis thought you must be an escaped prisoner."

"And you thought I was a fugitive?"

"I thought you might be. Richard thinks you're an author. We found some of your writing, you see. Are you an author, Fin?"

"I write," he said, pushing his big hat on to the back of his head. "But that's not always the same thing as being an author."

"You don't live here, do you?" I went on. "Henrietta says there isn't any water in the well."

"No, there isn't," he said. "I guess I'm just staying. It's a quiet sort of cabin, and suits me nicely."

"Are you writing a book?"

"That's the idea, Jep."

"It's about Canada, isn't it?"

He nodded.

"Penny was awfully interested too. She found the loose brick, otherwise they wouldn't have believed me. Francis is awfully suspicious by nature."

"I'm getting a bit muddled," Fin said suddenly. "You've mentioned Richard, and Francis, and Henrietta, and Penny. Is it some kind of a family you've inherited?"

I explained the whole lot of them to him more carefully.

"Well, I'm glad you've found some friends," he said. "Have you been here long?"

"No, but I want to stay," I said. "I like it here."

And then I told him a bit about my life, and all the dull places I had been to, and the heaps of silly people there are in the world. Fin agreed with me about silly people, and because he was so easy to talk to, and seemed so awfully interested in everything I had to say, I told him about my nature books, and how much I liked Henrietta, and even about my tropical fever. When I had stopped, because there didn't seem to be anything left to tell him, he just sat looking into the fire for a long time without speaking.

After a bit he put away his pipe and suggested we should go out for a walk.

"We'll go up the hill," he said. "There won't be a view to-day because of the mist, but something rare and exciting usually turns up on Raywhistle Brow."

The sun was almost visible through the mist when we reached the top of a high hump of ground about a quarter of a mile behind the cottage.

"Is this Raywhistle Brow?" I asked, panting a bit because Fin's legs are awfully long, and I should think he was always used to walking quickly.

"Yes. You get a grand view on a clear day, but I like it all ways up here. Look at those trees in the mist; kind of mysterious, aren't they?"

I looked and nodded, because I like it "all ways" too.

It was awfully quiet up there. The mist seemed to wrap up all sounds as well as sights, and I couldn't hear anything except my own heart beating. And then, very faint at first, we both heard something else. It sounded rather like a pack of hounds in full cry a long way off, and I suddenly felt Fin grip hold of my shoulder.

"We're in luck, Jep. Keep your eyes skinned," he said, and we both turned round towards the sound. It came nearer and nearer, wild, mysterious music, and somehow awfully lonely-sounding, then out of the mist directly in front of us, in a huge V across the sky came a skein of about thirty wild geese. They soared over our heads, so low that we could feel the rush of air made by their great wings, then away into the gloom behind us. Neither of us spoke until their sad music had died into silence, then Fin said, "Pinkfeet; but perhaps you knew."

Well, I didn't know, because I didn't know hardly anything about wild geese then.

"Where do they come from?" I asked, a bit breathless from the thrill of it all. "I've never seen them before."

"They breed up in the islands of the Arctic Sea," he said, "but just now they're down south at their winter feeding grounds. I guess the cold weather drove them inland a bit, and now they're off back to some river estuary."

"When do they go home, Fin?"

"Round about the end of February. Something just stirs within them, and suddenly they're all up and away with the dawn. I saw it happen once. It kinda got me, here!" He slapped his chest with his hand.

I knew what he meant, because it had kind of got me too, just to see and hear them going over.

As we walked away from the Brow he told me about other sorts of wild geese: barnacle, and brent, and greylag, all such lovely names.

"Out west we have our own Canadian species as well," he said, "and of course there's the snow goose."

"There's such a lot I want to know about birds," I said. "I've got some good books, but I've never found anyone before who really cares."

"We'll have to make some plans," Fin said. "You

must let me come along and meet your aunt some-
time."

"I'm afraid she might think it a bit queer," I said.
"I mean, me finding you in an empty cottage—and,
well, in those clothes. She's a bit fussy sometimes."

"Then we'll have to think of something else, won't
we."

"Could you write?" I suggested. "Say you are
staying near, or something?"

"Yes. I could do that, then smarten up a bit if she
asked me to call. Take off the old buckskin, and put
on a respectable tweed!"

"I think that might be best, if you wouldn't mind,"
I said. "But *I* like the buckskin best. Why do you
wear it, Fin?"

"It's windproof, and comfortable," he said. "I got
the hat from a Mounty."

"What's that?"

"He's a chap who belongs to the Royal Canadian
Mounted Police—fine fellows all of them, and I
reckon their hats make good umbrellas when it
rains!"

We reached the cottage and went inside.

"Don't you ever lock it, Fin?" I asked. "It was
open the day we came, and I'm afraid we just walked
in."

"That's O.K. Jep," he said. "Up in the north of
Canada you never lock the door of your shack.
Anybody can come in and spend the night provided
he leaves it just as he found it. That's the code up
there, and it's only when somebody breaks it that the
trouble begins."

We sat down and talked some more, then he said, "Look here Jep, I want just two more days on my own. There's a little job of writing I must get finished."

I frowned a bit: "It's the others, you see," I said, and I told him about my pretended headache.

He laughed and said: "Couldn't you make it last until the day after to-morrow?"

"I could," I said, "but I'm afraid they might tell Uncle Clive. He's a doctor, you see."

"Oh, that might be awkward. Then why not tell them the truth?"

"Francis will be mad—I don't think he likes me much. But perhaps it would be better to tell them. All right, Fin, I will."

He came with me as far as the gate into the wood.

"It's been a good day, Jep," he said, "and the first of many, I hope."

Then he called out after me as I went down the path, "Good luck. Hope you can make your peace with Francis!"

59

CHAPTER SEVEN

BATTLE WITH FRANCIS

IT turned out another fine day, and much warmer, although there was still quite a bit of snow about where the drifts had been deep. They were all dressed up and ready to start when I turned up at their house, and Beaver was bounding about in a state of great excitement.

"Got any special plans for us to-day, Jep?" Richard asked.

Well, now was my chance. "Yes, I have actually. Rather important plans," I said.

"What are they?" Francis said suspiciously.

"We're not going to the cottage to-day after all."

"Why ever not?" He shot me a very hostile look, which gave me that prickly fierce-bull feeling, but all the same I'd got to tell them.

"Because the Fugitive said so."

We were crossing a field behind the house, a stubbly field with the ground still hard in lumps from the frost, and they all stopped dead and stared at me.

"How do you mean?" Richard asked, frowning a bit.

"I saw him yesterday," I said, looking at my feet. "I didn't have a headache at all. It was just an excuse. You see, he'd *told* me to come alone so what else could I do?"

Well, I guessed that Francis would take it badly,

but I wasn't expecting what I got next. I wasn't even looking up when I felt his fist punch into my face. It made me bite my lip badly, and I suddenly saw red—real red like a huge glowing fire, and I jolly well let him have it back. I don't know how long we were at it before Richard got in between us, and sent Francis sprawling back one way and me the other. The ground was beastly hard and gave me a whole lot more bruises, and I was just going to get at Francis again when I felt someone's arms go round my chest pinning my arms to my side.

"Stop it, Jep!" Penny's voice said shrilly immediately behind me, and then I saw that Richard was holding Francis in the same way.

I remember noticing with satisfaction that his nose was bleeding, before I wrenched myself free from Penny's arms and bolted away across the field, my head humming like a bee's nest. I could hear Penny and Francis shouting at each other, and then I heard running footsteps behind me as Richard caught me up.

"I say, Jep, come back," he said. "Where are you off to?"

Well, I hadn't really thought! Aunt June would have had a fit if she'd seen me like that, for I could feel blood running down my chin and one of my eyes was bunging up.

"You haven't told us anything properly," he went on. "What's it all about anyway?"

"He didn't give me a chance——" I began indignantly.

"I know. Francis is an ass; it's his red hair."

Richard's placid voice calmed me down a bit, and

I began to feel rather foolish. We went back to the others, and he and Penny put handfuls of snow on our faces to try and stop the bruises coming up, and after a bit Francis ceased to hiss like a steam engine. Then when we both complained that our faces were getting frostbitten, they stopped their first aid, and Penny said:

"Anyway you both look perfectly frightful, whatever we do, and I don't know what they're going to say at home."

We didn't know either, and it might be a bit awkward to explain away because so far only Henrietta knew about the keeper's cottage.

"I think we ought to go back and tell her what's happened before Mummy and Daddy come in," Penny suggested. "She's good at making excuses for us, and she might make up something reasonable for Miss Henson too."

So we went back, and while Henrietta tried something else on our faces I told them nearly everything, but not who Fin really was; I wanted to keep that glorious secret to myself a little bit longer.

"And we want *you* to make excuses for the boys' faces, Henrietta," Penny said, looking at us. "They don't look too good, do they? Can't you make those bumps go down?"

"No," Henrietta said, "and I'm not making any excuses for anyone, either."

"But what shall we say?"

"Just that you've had a fight. After all, you did, didn't you? That's pretty obvious!"

We were all a bit silent for a moment, and then suddenly Penny burst out laughing.

"Jep's going to look just like a panda in the morning when his eyes go black, and Francis, *you* look just like a clown now. Your nose is bright red and twice the size!"

"He didn't hit me as hard as I did him," Francis said. "He hasn't got the strength."

"Haven't I then. You wait!" I said.

"Well, I've got some work to do," Henrietta said. "And if anyone wants me during the next hour, I'm out."

I felt quite important leading them up to Fin's cottage the next afternoon, but when we got there, although the door was wide open, nobody seemed to be about.

"Fooled again!" Francis said. "We might have known it."

"Don't be an ass," Richard said. "He must be somewhere or the door wouldn't be open."

"There's probably a sign telling us what to do," I said. "P'rhaps we've got to meet him somewhere."

So we all began to play hunt-the-sign, upstairs and downstairs, then outside as well.

"What are we looking for, anyway?" Francis said aimlessly, kicking a lump of snow about. Then suddenly he stopped and stared down at a patch of snow under the wall which hadn't quite melted away.

"Hi! Come and have a look at this," he called out. "Someone's been writing in the snow."

We all bunched up round him, and Richard read out slowly, pronouncing each letter: " 'Ckab ni a tomnem.' "

63

"It's Latin," Penny said hopefully. "Translate it, Richard."

"It's not Latin, silly," he said, frowning at the writing.

"Then it's a trap," Francis said, always suspicious of everything, but I guessed at once that it was a code, and very soon I had puzzled it out too.

"It means 'back in a moment'," I said.

Richard got it almost as quickly as I did, but the others were still puzzled.

"How?" Francis said. "What language?"

"Red Indian," said a deep voice behind us, and we all swung round to find Fin standing on the path and smiling at us.

Well, I knew what he looked like already, but the others seemed awfully impressed as they stood there and stared at him.

"Are you a Red Indian?" Penny asked suddenly. "You do look a bit like one."

"I was for a time," he said, and then I saw him looking at my and Francis's faces.

"What the dickens have you two chaps been up to?" he asked laughing.

Francis put his hand over his nose, and mine went up gingerly to my juicy black eye. We looked at each other rather sheepishly.

"They had a row yesterday," Richard said.

"And it was about you," Penny added.

Fin raised an eyebrow, but made no further comment then, and I thought Francis looked rather relieved.

"Well, it's nice to meet you all," he said, slinging

64

his pack in at the cottage door. "There goes our tea till we've earned it."

"How are we going to earn it?" Penny asked.

"We're going to do something mightily constructive I hope," he said, and then because we all looked puzzled he went on, "Seems I'd better explain myself. I care a lot about this little cabin, so I thought I'd best set about buying it."

"And did you?" Penny asked excitedly.

"Yes. It's all mine now, and I got it for not much more than a song because of the water."

"But I thought there wasn't any water?" Richard said.

"There isn't, at least not in the old well. But we're going to see what we can do about it this afternoon."

"How?" Francis asked.

"Find some water?" I suggested.

"Dig for it?" Richard added.

"Certainly, but not yet. It's a mug's game to dig for water which isn't there, don't you agree?"

"Er-yes," Richard said, "what are you going to do then? Bore through the earth's crust and discover an artesian well or a geyser or something?"

"Yes. Something like that." He looked at Richard and winked. "Now, come on. Quick march!" And he turned on his heel and set off towards the wood.

I hurried up beside him. "Fin, have you really bought the cottage?" I asked.

"Yes. Honest Injun!"

"Then—are you going to *live* here?"

"That's the idea, all being well with the water situation. Any objections?"

"Oh, no! I'm frightfully glad," I said. "You'll

E

only be about a mile from Aunt June and me, you know."

He looked down from his terrific height, and gave me a jolly nice smile as he said, "That was the chief attraction."

Then he lowered his voice a bit, and added, before the others caught us up, "Did you manage to make your peace with Francis?"

"I don't know," I said. "Richard stopped us in the middle. I don't think I did really."

CHAPTER EIGHT

THE DOWSERS

FIN led us into an avenue of hazel trees which arched together over our heads making a sort of tunnel, and he began to search with his hands among the supple branches. We watched him select a Y-shaped twig and slash it neatly off with one stroke of his knife.

"What's that for?" Penny asked. "Magic?"

"I shan't believe it if it is," Francis said firmly. "There isn't such a thing as magic, and even conjuring tricks can be explained if you know how."

"I promise you it isn't a conjuring trick," Fin said. "Now, right about turn, everyone."

I had an idea what Fin was going to do, and Richard looked as if he had guessed too, but neither of us let on to the others. We marched back to the piece of gently sloping ground behind the cottage, and Francis was beginning to look ferocious because he can't bear being teased, and obviously Fin was pulling his leg a bit.

"Now let's weave our magic spell," he said, suddenly stopping dead.

"Magic is supersonic rot!" Francis muttered to himself, but Fin heard him.

"We'll see," he said. "You just watch this little rod, Francis. It is going to tell me quite clearly if there's any underground water about."

"But it's only a stick. I saw you cut it."

"And full of magic powers. Mind you watch carefully!" He winked at us, and then held out the rod in both hands and began to walk slowly across the expanse of rough ground.

Everyone got suddenly very quiet, and I could only hear the wind sighing faintly in the tree tops as we stood there watching him.

After a bit the hazel twig began to twitch and bend in his hands, and it looked as if something invisible was pulling his arms downwards towards the earth. I had heard of water-divining but had never seen it done before, and there was something almost supernatural about it.

Francis looked furious. "You're just acting," he called out. "Anyone could do that."

"Is there water there?" Richard asked, ignoring his brother, and Fin nodded, walking back over the same piece of ground again.

"Yes. There's water down here all right," he said, as the little twig twitched and bent once more. "Who wants to see if they can dowse as well?"

Of course we all wanted to try, all except Francis who just didn't know how to take it! So the three of us had a go in turn, but nothing happened; the twig just lay lifeless in our hands. It was a bit of a disappointment.

"Well Francis, that only leaves you," Fin said. "What about it?"

"It's rot!" Francis retorted. "You all look mad."

"Nothing to what you look," Richard said. "Go on, be a sport. I think we'd die of laughter if *you* turned out to be a dowser!"

Francis snatched the stick angrily out of Richard's hands.

"Steady does it," Fin said, laying a hand on each of his shoulders. "Now just relax, and set off slowly. If you feel any pulling don't try to fight against it."

It was obvious to all of us after only a few seconds that Francis did feel some pulling, because his face went as red as a beetroot in his useless efforts to keep the little stick steady in his hands. It twitched and bent and pulled, and suddenly with an exasperated cry he flung it on to the ground.

None of us quite knew what to say, because it didn't seem fair somehow that he should be the lucky one, not that he looked very lucky just then, because his face was all screwed up and he was holding his wrists as if they were hurting him.

Then suddenly Richard began to die of laughter! Fin joined in, and then Penny and me, and after a bit even Francis too—he just couldn't help himself, and a green woodpecker flew over our heads from the wood laughing like mad as well. It was really frightfully funny! When we had calmed down a bit Francis said:

"But nobody's proved there's water down there, have they? It might be some sort of magnetic power from the moon. Perhaps I've got space magnetism!"

Fin laughed. "Good old Francis. You deserve to get to the moon." Then he took his wrists between his hands and rubbed them gently. "You shouldn't try to fight against nature. I warned you, didn't I?"

69

"You said it was magic," Francis said, "but there isn't such a thing as magic, is there? What happened? Why did I tingle like that?"

"I guess you've just got the gift," Fin said. "Some have and some haven't. It's nature's way."

"What did it feel like?" Penny asked.

"Jolly strong," Francis said, beginning to feel important. "The whole thing seemed to twist round in my hands—I couldn't stop it, and I had prickles all up my arms like an electric shock. I say, aren't we clever, Fin!"

"Well, nobody's *proved* there's water down there, have they?" he teased him. "Come on, let's get in to tea. I'm hungry."

"But aren't we going to dig now?"

"No spades, and not much daylight left to-day," he said, "but we do need a bit of firewood if anyone feels useful."

Fin had a marvellous tea ready for us when we came in with the wood, and while we ate it we got him to tell us a bit more about dowsing.

"Is it still used to-day for finding water?" Richard asked. "I mean, it seems a bit primitive for these scientific days, doesn't it?"

"Yes, it's still used," Fin said, "and it's true to say that dowsers have succeeded where geologists have failed."

"What's a geologist?" Francis wanted to know.

"Someone who studies the science of the earth's strata, isn't it?" Richard said, looking at Fin. "The crusty part before you get down to the red hot lava and fiery furnaces!"

"Don't let's talk about geologists," Penny said.

70

"Tell us about Red Indians, Fin. It's much more interesting."

"Did you live with them when you were in Canada?" Richard asked.

"Yes, for a time. They were mighty suspicious of me at first, like Francis, but we got friendly in the end."

"Did you sleep in a wigwam?" Penny said.

"Yes, some of the time."

"And did you always travel with sledge dogs?"

"In the winter yes, but in summer it's mostly canoes. Over the lakes when you come to them, then through the forests with your canoe on your back till you get to the next bit of water."

"Have you ever shot the rapids?" Francis asked.

"Oh yes. That's the very quickest way of travelling."

"What's it like? Do tell us."

"Well, it's exciting—and it can be dangerous too. If you happen to capsize your boat in the middle of those angry waters, you're as good as a dead man at once."

"Goodness! Aren't you frightened?" Penny said.

"I guess one gets too excited to be scared. You've only got to hear the thunder of those great waters, and feel the spray coming up fresh in your face to forget all about the danger of it—it kinda goes to your head like wine."

"Did you ever capsize?" Francis wanted to know.

"Yes, I did once. It must have been quite an amusing exhibition," and Fin laughed at the memory of it. "I was having a nice little three-mile trip down a particularly lively stretch of river, the sort with jagged bits of rock sticking up in all the wrong places—and I was doing fine; quite the old seasoned canoeman, I thought myself, kneeling up in the correct style and manœuvring my paddle from side to side. Then suddenly—woops! over went the whole contraption and me with it."

"Could you swim?" Penny asked anxiously.

"Yes, but it's not much use to you in that kind of water."

"Then whatever happened?" Francis said.

"Well, I didn't lose my canoe," Fin went on. "I clung on to it like a limpet, and down we went together! 'You've had it, Finlay Mackay,' I said to myself, and I guess I just shut my eyes and gave up. When I opened them again I was surrounded by a ring of dark trees, and the sun up above them was shining down warm and golden on to my face. 'Heaven,' I said to myself, 'that's where you've got to, Heaven!' Then I thought maybe I wasn't good enough to get up to that place so easily, and anyway there seemed a bit too much water around me for it to make sense."

"Where were you, Fin? Had somebody rescued you?"

"No. I was just lying on the bottom of a shallow pool with barely six inches of water covering me. Every rapid ends off in a pool somewhere or other, and this one was my salvation, so I just got up and walked home."

"Did you lose your canoe?"

"No, I got it back, but with a two-foot gash right

72

through the birch bark, the work of some sharp piece of rock."

"Lucky it wasn't your head," Penny said soberly.

"Yes, wasn't it, although I didn't get away entirely unscathed. That would be asking too much of those mischievous waters." He took off his jacket and rolled up one of his shirt sleeves, revealing a long white scar between his wrist and elbow.

"Golly!" Francis said. "I bet some blood came out of that!"

"It did. The pool was crimson!" Fin said with a laugh.

"Did you ever see a man drowned?" Francis asked hopefully, and he seemed quite disappointed when Fin said that he never did.

He talked more about the country of the Indians then, and about the great pine forests which come right down to the edge of the lakes, so dense with trees that they look quite black. He told us about the Indian drums which you can hear beating out in the evenings.

"A queer, unearthly sound among the trees, travelling clearly for miles, but I could never make out just where the sound was coming from."

"Did you like the country, Fin?" Penny asked. "It sounds a bit mysterious to me."

"Mysterious, and wild, and friendly, all in patches," he said, "but always beautiful in a vast, majestic kind of way."

"Didn't you hate leaving it all?" Richard said quietly.

"I got what I wanted—and more besides," Fin said, taking out his tobacco pouch and beginning to fill his pipe. "And now I've got to write it all down. That was the great idea."

"Why didn't you write it all down out there?" Penny asked.

"I guess I was homesick for the old country. Besides," he turned his head suddenly in my direction and gave me a colossal wink, "I had a good reason for coming home."

"What reason?" they all said at once.

"I've got a boy!"

This caused quite a stir, and I was glad it was dark enough inside the cottage for no one to be able to see my face properly.

"Have you got a wife then?" Francis said brightly.

Fin laughed. "Not yet, but there's always hope."

"But what sort of a boy is he, Fin?" Penny asked.

"Just an ordinary one—two arms, two legs, one nose——"

"But where is he?" Penny said, laughing. "I believe you're only teasing us."

"Maybe I am!" Fin took a glowing stick from the fire and lit his pipe, and soon the room was full of that queer, strong smell which had first guided me to the cottage. "And maybe I'm not," he added.

Then he told us that this was proper Red Indian tobacco, and that he only smoked it in private because of the smell.

"I like it," Richard said. "It's a good sort of smell." Then suddenly he noticed that it was almost dark outside. "Gosh, Fin. We ought to be going home, you know. What time can we come to-morrow?"

"As early as you like. We've got a whole day's work in front of us."

We walked home in the dark with a bit of moon showing up above the pine trees, and I don't think we quite knew which country we were really in, England or Canada. At the top of the lane above Blue Gates he halted.

"See you in the morning," he said, "and don't forget to bring along those spades. Good night now."

We all said "Good night", and thanked him for everything, then turned to give a last wave of good-bye. But Fin just wasn't there. He had slipped back into the darkness with the silence and stealth of a wild animal, or like a Red Indian perhaps!

CHAPTER NINE

THE PEACE PIPE

"HOW long d'you think this is going to take?" Francis asked, digging his iron spade deep into the rough ground and turning up a spadeful of root-infested soil.

"Depends how far down the spring is, and how hard we work," Fin said, the enormous spade he had got hold of throwing up as much of the earth in one go as all of us put together.

"Jolly lot of roots and things down here," Richard remarked. "This one feels as hard as a stone— wow! it is a stone."

We had dug down quite far now, good old Beaver helping us like mad at intervals, and had made a sort of trench about four foot long and two foot wide when the soil suddenly became stony.

"Was there a quarry here, or something?" Richard wondered.

"I hope not," Fin said. "Out you get, all of you, and let me have a look."

He had put a wooden board against the side of the pit to prevent the walls from falling in, and we all clambered over it on to the grass.

"Is this how you dig a grave?" Penny asked.

"I don't know, Penny, I've never dug one," Fin said. "Here, catch these stones and stack 'em up somewhere."

76

He threw them up to us like builders do with bricks, and we had some fun catching and dropping them! We had made quite a big pile of flattish grey stones before he got down to softer earth again underneath.

"We'd better work in shifts now," he said, "two at a time for ten minutes each. It's getting a bit cramped for all five."

Things began to happen during mine and Penny's second shift together. Francis was getting more and more unbelieving, because we had got down quite far now without finding even the suspicion of a spring. Fin had said that the ground would begin to get soggy and only a small muddy puddle would appear at first, so you can imagine my surprise when the ground suddenly gave way beneath me, and half my body seemed to fall through into space. I shouted to Penny, who was up at the other end of the trench, to look out, and saw her scrambling up the wall as I got my spade shaft across the hole and clung on to it for dear life!

The other two had been up the hill with Fin, but at Penny's shouts for help they came racing down to the rescue. Fin lifted me out, spade and all, with one great heave, and still holding me firmly by the shoulders he stared down into the pit. We all looked, for the hole made by my body was slowly widening as the earth trickled through it like sand in an hour-glass.

"Listen!" Fin said suddenly. "Do you hear that?" We all listened, and from far below us came the plop-plop sound of something falling into water.

"It's a hidden well," Richard said excitedly.

"Yes." Fin looked a bit shaken, I thought, and come to think of it it might have been a bit awkward if I'd fallen right through!

"A nice muddy puddle, I don't think!', Francis said sarcastically, and I felt like shoving him down the well.

"But why was it all covered up?" Penny asked.

"I can't imagine," Fin said. "Somebody's daft idea!"

"Perhaps it's stagnant water," Richard suggested. "It sounded miles and miles down. Good job you didn't go right in, Jep."

"It would have been frightful," Penny said with a shudder. "Could we have got him up again, Fin?"

But Fin didn't seem very interested in what might have happened.

"We'd best get a can and some rope and have a look at it," he said. "You'll find both in the cabin."

It was only then that I realized one of my boots had gone. I can't think why none of us had noticed it before, and of course we laughed like anything.

"And I doubt if we can get it up again very easily, Jep," Fin said.

"I'll go back and get another pair, shall I?" Richard suggested. "You can't very well just hop around for the rest of the day."

It was awfully decent of him, but seemed rather hard luck him having to go all that way for me. By the gate into the wood he turned and shouted, "Can I bring Henrietta if she's not busy?"

We all shouted back "Yes", and Fin added,

"Your lunch too. It looks as though we'd got a day's work in front of us."

We fetched the things from the cottage, and Fin showed us the proper way to attach the rope to the handle.

"A round turn and two half hitches," he said. "That's twice round the handle, then a clove hitch on to the rope. The handle takes all the strain then so that it's easy to untie. There!" He tied it neatly in about a second.

"Were you a Scout?" Penny asked.

"I was."

"Richard is too."

"Then I guess he'd have known this little knot. Now, down she goes."

He let the can gently through the hole, and after a bit we heard a faint splash as it reached the water below. Then he laid his spade across the trench and made me and Francis hold it steady. He let Penny haul it up again, gently hand over hand till the can came into sight, toppling a bit, and brim full of water.

"Does it smell?" Francis said, as Fin put down a long arm and lifted it carefully on to the grass.

We all peered inside, and except for a bit of soil which had fallen in, the water looked as clear and crystal as a spring. Beaver came panting back from a rabbit chase, and put out a long thirsty tongue to lap it up.

"He thinks it's good anyway," Fin laughed. "But we'd best get it analysed first."

"What's that?" Francis said.

"Looking for germs, isn't it?" Penny said, "and seeing what it's made of."

"But water isn't made of anything," Francis declared. "How could it be? It's just water."

"It's a liquid compound of oxygen and hydrogen; what the scientists call H_2O; melting point $0°$ centigrade, boiling point $100°$ centigrade, and a gallon of water weighs 10 pounds—in case you want to know," Fin remarked with a laugh. "And it could be full of bacteria—cocci, bacilli and spirilla, so we're not taking any risks."

Well, that silenced Francis all right. He just had nothing to say back. Fin is the only person I know who can put Francis in his place, but they're jolly good friends all the same.

Richard came back with the boots while we were busy clearing the mouth of the well. It had to be boarded over after that, and a fence built up all round it, and when Henrietta arrived later with our lunch we were all hot and dirty and quite ravenous. Fin hauled up a lot more water for us to wash in, but he wouldn't let any of us drink it yet.

"I've got a supply of corporation water in the cabin for that," he said, "all carried by hand, so it's valuable!"

Henrietta obviously approved of the cottage, and of Fin too, but she didn't seem keen about the way he was living—sleeping on the floor and all that.

"A bit primitive, isn't it?" she said. "I mean, you haven't got any comforts at all as far as I can see."

"Well, it isn't exactly the Ritz!" he replied, smiling, "but I guess I'm used to this sort of life."

"Why couldn't *we* have him till this place is done up?" Penny said suddenly, but Fin only laughed again and shook his head.

"Thanks a lot, Penny, but this is my home now. By the way, what shall we call it?"

"It used to be the keeper's cottage," Richard said, "but that wouldn't suit you, Fin, I mean, you're not a bit like a keeper."

We all tried various things. Penny wanted it to be "Jep" of all the daft names, and Francis suggested "The Moon Rocket" after his beloved space ships. I thought about "The Log Cabin"—not that it was built of logs, but because of Fin and Canada, and Henrietta and Richard both thought it ought to be something to do with water. So in the end we decided on "The Well Cabin" and I think it will be called that now for always.

Fin didn't hurry us back to work again after we had eaten absolutely everything Henrietta had provided, but let us just sit about on the floor and talk.

"When the fire goes out we'll go out too," he said, throwing on another handful of wood chippings.

We watched them leap into flame, hissing and spitting a bit.

Then suddenly Penny said, "Fin, do tell us about your boy, please."

"What boy?" Henrietta asked, looking interested.

"He says he's got one, and that's why he came home from Canada but he won't tell us properly. Oh Fin, *please!*"

Well, it obviously had to come some time, so when Fin cocked an eye at me for advice, I just nodded.

F

He made a terrific story of it which kept them all mystified till the end. I think they thought he must have adopted a Red Indian boy or something, because he made an awful lot of my woodcraft and out-of-door life, talking about blazing trails and Red Indian signs and things.

"But where is he *now*?" Penny asked. "What have you done with him?"

"He's sitting right by your side at this very moment, and if I'm not mistaken, very pleased to have made your acquaintance."

Well, they all blew up then, Francis just like a squib and on top of me too, sitting right on my stomach and punching my head. I couldn't heave him off because he weighed half a ton, but I got my fists into his middle all right which made him double up and roll over, then we both scrambled up into better fighting positions.

Fin's living-room isn't very big, and there were six of us and the dog in it already, but I wasn't going to let Francis get away with these unprovoked attacks! We fell over Penny, and knocked down a couple of thermos flasks, and Beaver got in between my feet, but I managed to get some good ones home before Fin picked us up by our collars—one in each of his hands, and dropped us outside on the grass.

"If you must fight, do it out here," he said, then he called the others back to work.

We stopped fighting then and joined them, but all the afternoon Francis kept glaring at me and I knew it wasn't properly over yet; one of us had got to win.

By tea-time our work was finished, and we were

all rather proud of the wooden fence which now surrounded our well.

I had almost forgotten about my row with Francis until Fin suddenly said, "Who wants the divining-rod as a keepsake?"

Then Francis and I both shouted out "Me!" at the same time, and raced over to the bush where Penny had hung it up.

"It isn't any good to you," Francis bellowed, "you haven't got the gift like me."

"And you said you didn't believe in it," I retorted, "and anyway I found Fin first."

"Yes, in a beastly sneaking sort of way——"

"Well, he's my Guardian, so there!"

We argued with words until there was nothing left to say, then we got down to business with our fists.

I heard Penny wail, "Oh, Henrietta, they've started again. *Do* stop them," and Fin telling her to let us fight it out. And we jolly well did too! It was the best fight I've ever had, and we only stopped in the end because neither of us could breathe any more.

The others were sitting round the fire when we came in, and there were two candles burning on the mantelpiece. It looked lovely and friendly, and I could smell cocoa cooking in Fin's billy can. Francis and I flopped down at the end of the circle, and Beaver came up and licked our faces. Henrietta held the mugs while Fin spooned in the cocoa and Richard passed them round.

Then Fin took out his pipe and filled it with Red Indian tobacco and lit it from a smouldering stick of pine wood. He seemed suddenly grave and important, and we all stopped talking and looked at him.

"Now then," he said, "we are going to smoke the pipe of peace, Red Indian fashion."

He puffed at it himself for a moment to get it going properly, and the room began to fill up with that familiar smell, then he solemnly passed it to Henrietta, who puffed too, and she passed it on to me, and so on all round the circle, and back again to Fin.

"The symbol of peace among tribes," he said in a slow, deliberate sort of way, "so there will be no more fighting in this forest now."

"O.K. Fin," Francis said, "there won't be any more. Jep and me can't beat each other anyway."

And he flung his arm over my shoulder. I knew it was meant as his own special symbol of peace, so I flung mine over his shoulder too, and we sat there like a couple of chimpanzees, savouring the extraordinarily bitter but exciting taste left in our mouths by the peace-pipe.

CHAPTER TEN

FIN COMES TO CALL

AUNT JUNE was very good at not asking what I had been doing, and as long as she knew I was with the Sorsbies she didn't seem to mind how long I stayed out. In fact I think she was a bit relieved to get me out of the way. A few mornings after we had smoked the pipe of peace, she came into my room with an open letter in her hand.

"Such an extraordinary thing, Jeffrey," she said. "I have just received a letter from Mr. Mackay, your Guardian. It seems he is back again in England, and staying quite near here."

"Gosh!" I said, trying to sound surprised. "What does he say?"

"He says he would like to come and visit us."

"Well, he can, can't he?"

"Yes, dear, I think he should come. After all, your parents left you legally in his care, and he certainly hasn't done very much about it, has he?"

"Oh! He couldn't help it, Aunt June—I mean, well, I'm sure he couldn't. I expect he was awfully busy. When d'you think he'll come?"

"Let me see? He suggests to-morrow afternoon. Dear me, that means I shall have to do some baking."

Well, that was that, and after breakfast I went

round to the Sorsbies' house and found them making all sorts of plans and preparations for Fin's comfort.

"Henrietta's got a bed and a table and a cupboard and a frying pan and a kettle and an arm-chair and *tons* of other things," Penny said, "and we're going to take it all over in Richard's trek cart now!"

Richard was awfully particular about packing up the trek cart so that it was properly balanced.

"You've got to remember that it's only got two wheels," he said, "and if you get all the weight one end and then go down or up a steep hill—well, you've had it!"

It was great fun and quite hard work, but we managed the journey all right with Richard telling us what to do. Francis and I took the shafts, and the rest of them hung on to the drag ropes and pulled with all their might, and then when we went down a hill Richard and Henrietta took the shafts, and we reversed the ropes to act as a brake. It was quite easy when we learnt how, and a jolly good way of carrying a lot of luggage over rough country.

Fin came out of The Well Cabin when he heard us arriving, and stood by the doorway watching. He's so tall that his head comes right up above the lintel.

"Say! What's all this?" he said, as we marched triumphantly up what had once been the garden path.

"The inside of your new house," Penny said. "Absolutely everything you could possibly want!"

We unknotted the big canvas rick-sheet which was holding everything together, and then we all helped to carry everything inside and arrange it about to make the place look homely.

"Where d'you want the bed, Fin?" Francis asked. "Upstairs or downstairs?"

"Upstairs certainly," he said, "and in the best bedroom, too. Come on up and I'll show you."

Henrietta and Penny got busy with scrubbing brushes and things then, and the rest of us went out to look at the well.

"Trust the women to think about dirt," Fin remarked with a smile. "But I guess the place could do with a clean out."

We stood round the good fence we had made, and looked down into the well.

"What will you do, Fin?" Richard asked, "use it as a well with a bucket and everything, or get it piped to the house?"

"I've got someone coming to look at it to-morrow morning," he said, "and if everything's O.K. I guess we'll get going with the pipe idea. Buckets and things have their romance, but it's nice to be able to turn on a tap all the same."

"Aunt June got your letter this morning," I said. "She's going to invite you to tea to-morrow."

"Doesn't she know, then?" Francis asked.

"Not yet," I said. "She never asks questions."

"So isn't told no lies!" Fin laughed. "How shall I turn up, Jep? In a Rolls Royce?"

"You don't look much like a millionaire," Francis said.

"That's true enough—no more am I. What about an aeroplane then, as if I'd just arrived from Canada?"

"Or a space ship," Francis put in.

"Why not borrow a horse?" Richard said suddenly, and Fin seemed delighted with this idea.

"Just the thing," he said, "if we can get hold of one. Behold! the country squire making a courtesy call on his ward's great-aunt!"

"She's *not* my great-aunt," I said laughing, but all the same we thought the country squire idea was a good one.

There was a terrific smell of soap and disinfectant in the Cabin when we got back, and Penny looked completely black all over.

"It was absolutely filthy, Fin," she said. "But you've got two clean rooms now anyway, so mind you wipe your feet when you come in!"

Henrietta didn't look very much cleaner than Penny, and she seemed quite hot and exhausted as if she'd been working frightfully hard. Fin made her some tea in his new kettle, and insisted that she should sit down in the best arm-chair. Then he sent us all into the wood—all except Henrietta—for half an hour, and told us to take a corner each and have an observation nature test.

"I've got a little prize here for the best one," he said, "and don't come back too soon!"

I was quite glad of this time alone, because what with one thing and another I hadn't done anything in my nature books for nearly a week. I was in luck, too. First I watched a green woodpecker tapping for insects in the trunk of a hollow beech tree, and then a big flock of wood pigeons wheeled down from the sky with a clatter of wings. Pigeons are terribly shy birds and it's only very occasionally that you get the luck to watch a flock of them feeding, so I pressed myself against the trunk of a tree and stayed quite still. And I must have looked a bit like the tree because a red squirrel suddenly sprang down from the branches above me, and paused for a moment actually on my shoulder to nibble at a hazel nut. But the crack of its sharp little teeth entering the shell made me jump, and in a flash it was up the tree again stamping indignantly with its front feet on the branch and uttering a little bark of protest at having been fooled. The pigeons flew off then with another great clatter of wings, and the squirrel dropped the nut on to my head. I stooped down and rescued it from the dead leaves, and put it in my pocket, then moved deeper in among the bushes.

The jays were busy squawking now at the other end of the wood, probably because of Francis's jolly bad stalking, and after a bit we met.

"Seen anything?" I asked him.

"A blackbird"

"Is that all?"

"I found this bit of wood," he said, holding it up proudly. "It's exactly the shape of a rocket."

Francis really is hopeless in some ways, but I suppose he can't help being mad on getting to the moon!

Penny was awfully excited because she had seen a stoat carrying a dead mole, and Richard's best observation was some hens' feathers near the mouth of a fox's earth, which told their own story.

"D'you think we can go back now?" Penny said. "Have we been half an hour yet?"

"Longer," Richard said. "I say, Jep, your squirrel will easily win the prize."

We all voted for the best one when we got back, and my squirrel did win. Fin gave me a little pocket compass.

"To tell the time by," he said, which surprised us all a bit!

"How d'you mean?" Francis asked.

"As long as you've got the sun as well it's quite simple," Fin told us. "You see, the sun's always due east at 6 a.m. except that you have to make allowances for summer time, and due west at 6 p.m., and south at midday. If you know that much you can work out the rest; just simple arithmetic."

"Arithmetic's *never* simple," Penny moaned. "But I see what you mean. Fin, how does a compass work?"

"It's not magic, anyway," Francis said, grinning.

"No," Fin remarked, holding it in the palm of his hand. "This card here is floating in liquid, and the little needle balancing in the middle of it is magnetized. If you hold it steady and let the needle go round freely, it always points to the magnetic north."

"I think men are awfully clever to be able to invent things like this, don't you?" Penny said.

"Yes, if they deserve all the credit, which they don't really," Henrietta put in quietly, and we all looked at her to see what she meant.

"It's discovering all the wonders of the universe which is really clever," she went on. "After all, the magnetic north, and iron having the properties of magnetism, were always there—just as electromagnetic waves were always floating about in the air until Marconi found out how to transmit them into wireless signals."

Penny looked thoughtful, sitting with her chin in her hands, and staring into the fire.

"You mean that God is the Great Inventor really," she said, "and men are just discoverers. Yes, of course it's like that if you come to think of it."

I looked at Fin to see how he was taking this, and found that he was looking at Penny in an interested sort of way.

"That's a very profound statement, young lady," he said. "I like it a lot."

"It was Henrietta's idea," Penny said. "The words just came into my head."

Fin handed back my compass then, and told us to go outside and find out the time.

The sun seemed to be exactly in the south-south-west, so we made it one-thirty p.m., and when we went in to tell them, Henrietta shot out of her chair and said we must go back to lunch at once.

"I'd no idea it was so late," she said. "The time's simply flown."

"Time's no object at The Well Cabin," Fin said with a laugh. "See you to-morrow for tea, Jep."

Well, by tea-time the next day I was getting quite jumpy, and so was Aunt June as well. She kept on saying silly things like, "Are you sure you have brushed your hair properly?" and "Don't forget your manners, Jeffrey," and I replied, "Yes, Aunt June," and "No, Aunt June," just like a kid at school!

It was nearly four o'clock when I heard horse's

hooves on the road outside, and rushed to the sitting-room window to look out. Yes, it was Fin all right, looking absolutely smashing on a great big chestnut horse. He was wearing proper riding clothes too, and although it wasn't quite so exciting as the buck-skins he did look awfully fine.

"Aunt June—come quick!" I called out, "I think he's arrived on a horse."

I wanted her to see him just like that before he dismounted.

"Dear me, Jeffrey, what a very handsome gentle-man," she said, going quite pink in the face. "I must go and put the kettle on at once."

"And I'll go and hold the horse," I said, which seemed a good idea because it meant that Fin and I wouldn't have to pretend we'd never met before, in front of Aunt June.

"Fin, what a marvellous horse!" I said, running my hand down his glossy neck. "Wherever did you get him?"

"Henrietta borrowed him for me. Do I look O.K.?"

"You look wonderful. Aunt June's all in a flap!" And I held the horse's head while Fin swung out of the saddle. "But I wish he belonged to you," I added.

"So do I. I guess he comes from one of the richest homes in this neighbourhood. Henrietta's certainly got a way with her."

We led the horse round to the back to tie him up, and give him a bucket of water to drink, then came round again to the front door. Fin's enormous height made Aunt June look simply tiny, but he was awfully polite to her, and the tea-party went off without a hitch.

"I understand that this is the best place my ward has stayed in yet," he said presently. "We both hope very much that you're prepared to keep him on for a time, Miss Henson?"

I held my breath then, and looked anxiously at Aunt June, because this was a matter of life or death to me.

"Oh, yes, Mr. Mackay," she said with a smile. "Jeffrey and I get on very well together, and I should like him to think of Blue Gates as his home as well as mine."

"Thanks awfully, Aunt June," I said, and Fin added:

"That's fine. We're very grateful to you." Then he took out his wallet and handed her a small white card, saying with a smile, "My future address, Miss Henson. And there's quite a story attached to it too. You must get Jep to tell you about it."

Aunt June put on her spectacles and looked at the card, and I peered over her shoulder.

"Finlay Mackay, The Well Cabin, Dinglewood Marsh", it said, and it was printed too. Fin was certainly determined to make a good impression.

But Aunt June looked puzzled. "Does Jeffrey know the story about it?" she asked.

"He does," Fin said with a laugh. "You know, Miss Henson, this boy's a dark horse. You have to squeeze him to get out his secrets!"

She looked up at me then, and I looked pleadingly at Fin, but he just laughed again and got up.

"Well, it's been very pleasant meeting you, and I

hope it will be the first of many. We're near neighbours now, you know."

"But I'm afraid I don't quite know where this house of yours is situated, Mr. Mackay," Aunt June said. "I have lived here for so many years, but have never come across that name before. Let me see, what was it?"

"The Well Cabin, Aunt June," I said.

"Jep will tell you," Fin said, shaking her by the hand. "And many, many thanks for your splendid tea. I've never met a better cook."

Well of course that bucked her up a lot, and we stood in the road watching him ride away. He rides awfully well, and at the corner he turned in the saddle and raised his whip to us.

"What a very charming gentleman," Aunt June said, "and such courtly manners. Quite like the old-fashioned country squire."

Well, that had gone off all right, and now I had got to do a bit of explaining I supposed.

"Do you want to hear about 'The Well Cabin', Aunt June?" I asked as we went indoors together.

She peered down at me sideways, like a thrush looking at a worm, then she smiled rather sweetly and said:

"I don't want you to tell me anything you do not wish me to know, dear."

Well, that settled it.

"I do want you to know," I said, and then I told her all the bits which really mattered.

CHAPTER ELEVEN

FULL MOON

IT was the night of the full moon that I had a bit of an adventure; not the criminal-detective sort that you read about in books, nor like those journeys into space that Francis is so mad about, but something which I shall always remember for the rest of my life.

I couldn't go to sleep somehow. The moon was so bright, and it seemed an awful waste of time to be just lying in bed when everything outside was awake and sparkling. So I got up and hung out of the window. It was really a wonderful night, so peaceful and quiet, with the great round moon up there giving a silvery light to the whole country-side.

Then I had an idea. I'd got to go to Fin; he wouldn't be asleep either on such a night, so why shouldn't we share it together?

It was frosty outside, but not too cold, and I was soon over the fields and through the wood, for I knew my way so well by then.

The Cabin stood in a pool of moonlight, a down-stairs window blinking a faint yellow light at me, and a pinnacle of smoke rose straight upwards from the chimney, telling me that Fin had not gone to bed either. I knocked twice, and heard a chair scrape backwards on the floor as Fin got up to answer it.

Then he opened the door, and stood there for a moment looking down at me.

"Hullo, Jep! Nothing wrong, I hope?"

"No," I said. "I just couldn't go to sleep."

"Neither could I." He stooped his head and came out through the doorway into moonlight, his long shadow falling suddenly across the path in front of me.

"Let's go into the wood," he said. "It's too good a night to miss."

We entered from the top this time through a gap in the bank, and Fin led the way down a narrow winding path among the trees till we came to a clearing. He walked as silently as a tiger, and neither of us spoke. It was quite dark among the trees, but the clearing was washed in silver light with bars of black shadows from the trees cutting across it. Fin skirted the pool of moonlight and led me into the gloom of a small grove of hazels.

"Make yourself comfortable," he said softly. "We may have to wait some time. There should be foxes about, and in that bank over there is a badger's set."

We waited, and the night noises of the wood crept into the silence around us; the rustle of a tiny animal moving, faint stirrings above us from a sleeping bird, the soft sigh of wind in the tall pines, and the sudden hoot of a hunting owl.

Then on the crisp, frosty ground we heard the quick pad-pad of springy footsteps and a big dog-fox trotted across the clearing, disappearing like a shadow among the trees, and the sharp yap-yap of its solitary bark drifted back to us through the darkness.

I nudged Fin's arm and whispered, "What's he up to?"

"Looking for a mate most likely," he murmured. "They pair off round about now, like all wild things."

Far away the church clock struck midnight, twelve sombre notes, and as the night breeze rose and died again in the tree tops we suddenly heard a new sound. It was the sighing, grunting noise of a badger leaving his set to roam abroad in search of food. We watched his broad grey body lumbering across the clearing like a small bear, and once he turned to sniff the air and amble back to the mouth of his home. He grunted down the big hole under the bank, then turned again and padded leisurely away out of sight along a well-worn track made hard and bare by his own feet.

Then silence came down over the whole wood, a silence so deep and unrevealing that when a vixen screamed suddenly from the path behind us I almost jumped out of my skin, and even Fin stirred a little uneasily.

"Eerie creatures, these she-foxes," he said with a low laugh.

"It's an awfully weird sound," I murmured. "Listen, Fin! Is that the dog-fox answering?"

Far away to our right came the sharp yap-yap again, then another cry, in front of us this time, and more barks from right and left until it seemed that the whole wood was suddenly full of foxes.

"Seems to be some competition going on," Fin said. "Let's leave them to it, shall we? I'm getting cramped."

"So am I," I said, stamping pins and needles out of one of my feet.

"We were lucky to see old brock to-night," Fin said, when we were out of the wood again. "I was afraid it might be too cold for him."

"Do badgers hibernate?"

"They have a special winter chamber low down in the set, and when food gets scarce because of the cold the whole family goes off to bed for a long sleep. There must be a warmer spell on the way to have woken him up."

"Badgers aren't vermin, are they, Fin?" I asked, remembering having seen a dead one once, hanging up in a farmyard.

"Not really, though I think the keepers aren't too pleased when old brock goes off with a clutch of partridge eggs. But then, he only shoots the badger so that he can rear the partridges to be shot in their turn. Seems a bit mad, doesn't it?"

I nodded. "Why do people like killing things, Fin?"

"I guess it's a sort of disease," he said. "Some people would shoot an archangel if they got the chance!"

"Do *you* want to kill things?"

"No. Let 'em live and study 'em alive is my motto, unless you do it for food only. I don't want to kill for pleasure."

"Nor do I," I said. "I can't see the point."

We got back to the cabin, and Fin blew the embers of fire into life again, and lit the stubs of candle on the mantelpiece.

"Did you notice the black and white stripes on the

badger's head?" he asked, "and how well they fitted
in with the moonlight?"

"Yes. That's nature's camouflage, isn't it?" I said.
"It's awfully clever."

"One of the many wonders," he said, puffing away
at his pipe.

I looked up at him across the flickering firelight,
at the lights and shadows playing on his face and the
hand which held his pipe, then I said quietly, "Fin,
do you believe in God?"

He nodded, gazing into the fire, "I guess I do,
Jep. When all's said and done it's the only thing,
really."

We sat there for a long time and talked about
many things. Fin told me a bit about my parents,
how my mother had been a musician, and my father
a great ornithologist—that's someone who studies
birds. It may seem funny to you, but I didn't know
either of these things because nobody had ever told
me before.

"Your father and I were great pals in our young
days, Jep, before I became a journalist and he went
off to Nigeria. We spent most of our holidays
together in those days."

"What did you do?" I asked.

"We walked and camped over all the best bits of
this country, and got ourselves acquainted with the
out-door world. He taught me a lot about all that
sort of thing."

"What did my father look like, Fin?"

"Quite a bit like you—dark hair and nice grey eyes,
and tall and straight like a tree."

"Was he as tall as you?"

Fin laughed. "Not quite. That's asking a lot, isn't it?"

It was funny to think that my father had been a bit like me; I had never thought about it before.

"What was my mother like?" I asked presently.

"She was beautiful, Jep—as lovely as a princess, and as kind-hearted as Henrietta."

"Henrietta's a bit beautiful too, isn't she?" I said.

"Yes, I guess she is," Fin said with a smile, "and in a lot of ways she's quite like your mother, too."

We were quiet after that, each with our own thoughts, and presently Fin said, "Does it ever seem strange not having your own folk, Jep?"

"Hardly ever," I said. "You see, I can't remember them. It was such ages and ages ago. But no one's ever told me about them before, and it is nice to know a little."

He was quiet again for a little while then, before he said, "Well, you've got me now for keeps, if I'm any sort of use as a substitute, though I guess I shouldn't have left you on your own so long. That was bad!" And he sounded so conscience-stricken that I went and sat down on his feet like a dog to show him that I didn't mind!

I think I must have got a bit sleepy after that, because I don't remember much until I found Fin shaking me gently by the shoulder.

"Three a.m. by the moon," he said. "Isn't it time you were going back?"

We walked back together, and he waited in the garden till I gave him the "all's well" from my bedroom window. Aunt June was still snoring away peacefully in her bed, and I was jolly soon in mine, and probably snoring too!

We were often over at The Well Cabin during the last weeks of the holidays. Work soon began on the new water system, and there was lots of painting and cleaning up to do inside to make the place decent to live in. They never found my boot, by the way, and Francis still swears that the water tastes of rubber!

Everybody seemed interested in Fin and his cabin, and they all came over to do things whenever they had time. Aunt June made all the new curtains, and Uncle Clive did lots of digging and put in plants from his own garden.

Francis and I set about making a new garden fence and gate, and we didn't do too badly with Fin as our foreman. We never fought now, not since we'd smoked the pipe of peace, although we did occasionally hit each other just for fun.

Then term time began, and I went off to school with the others every day. It seemed a pretty decent sort of school too, and of course there was every evening and week-end free—except for a bit of sloppy homework, and I managed to get over to The Cabin quite often. Fin and I started up a joint nature record, like he and my father used to keep, he said. Spring's a wonderful time for records, and we soon began to get all sorts of exciting entries.

By the Easter holidays Fin's cabin was almost finished and his own furniture had arrived from London. I don't think the days had ever felt so long or so glorious as they did that April, and I had a sort of feeling that they might go on for ever like that. Everything seemed just about as perfect as it could have been, and there was Fin settling himself down for good only about a mile away from us.

And then something happened—at least it was the result of something we did, and I thought it was going to wreck everything.

CHAPTER TWELVE

SHOOTING THE RAPIDS

IT was Sunday, Palm Sunday, and after having come to church with us in the morning Fin shut himself up in The Cabin with his writing, and we all promised to leave him in peace for the rest of the day. It was an absolutely smashing day, the bluest sky you can imagine, and really warm sun, and flowers and birds everywhere. Aunt June and I often had Sunday dinner with the Sorsbies now, and during the meal Richard suddenly said, "Let's pack up some grub and go out for the rest of the day."

We all said "Good idea", then looked at the grown-ups, but they thought that it was a good idea too. So we simply dashed through the washing-up, and only broke one thing (it was Francis really but he said it was my fault) and managed to be ready to start soon after two o'clock.

"Don't forget your macs," Henrietta said. "You know what April is!" but we seemed to have got so much to carry already that only Richard took her advice.

"Where are you going?" Aunt Bridget asked.

"We're not sure, Mum," Richard said, "but we'll probably start off by the river."

"And discover its source," Penny said. "I've always wanted to do that."

"And we probably won't be back till it's dark,"

Francis said, swinging a haversack of food on to his back.

"Mind you don't get lost," Aunt June said, and Uncle Clive called after us as we started down the garden:

"Look out for crocodiles!"

Richard had the biggest pack to carry. It was absolutely bulging, and he had got his Scout staff as well.

"What have you got in there?" Penny wanted to know.

"Things we might need," he said, "and I hope you've got your compass, Jep, because I've left my watch behind on purpose. We're going to be proper pioneers."

"Yes, I've got it," I said, because I always took it everywhere.

We soon got to the river, and then walked beside it for miles, through copses, and over meadows and ploughed fields. Penny found the first buttercup, and we crossed a water meadow full of marsh marigolds and cuckoo flowers, then climbed underneath a bridge and I saw a kingfisher for half a second as it flashed round the bend. We went through a village, and past a watermill, then out into wilder country again with hills and woods all round us, and the river looked broader and deeper now, and somehow more exciting. Suddenly Richard stopped.

"Has anyone realized anything?" he said.

"What about?"

"About the river."

We all looked down into it.

"Oh! Yes," I said, "it's flowing the same way as

we are walking. I thought we were going to discover
its source?"

"We'll end up in the sea if we go on at this rate!"
Richard said with a laugh. "Nice pioneers we'd
make, I don't think!"

"Well, anyway it doesn't matter," Penny said.
"Let's go into those woods over there."

They were lovely woods, and the river ran right
through the middle of them. On one side the trees
were beech and oak mostly with just a sprinkling of
new leaves coming out on some of the lower branches,
and on the other side they were chiefly conifers,
with a lovely patch of fresh green larch. I think
larch is almost my favourite tree, especially in the
spring.

"I'm hungry," Francis said. "Is it nearly tea-
time?"

I got out my compass and we all looked at it.

"The sun's about half-way between south-west,
and west-south-west," I said. "What does that
make it?"

"Round about 4 o'clock," Richard said. "Let's
get a fire going and boil the kettle."

"Have we really been walking for two hours?"
Penny said. "I'm not a bit tired."

She and Richard got the fire going down by the
river away from the trees, and while we were waiting
for the kettle to boil Francis and I did a bit of exploring. There had been a lot of tree felling going on
higher up the wood, and logs of wood lay about
everywhere, some neatly stacked and ready for haul-
ing, and others just higgledy-piggledy all over the
place.

Richard's voice called out from below that tea was ready, and we raced down the slope to have it. It was lovely down by the river, sunny and sort of clean everywhere, with a faint smell of wood-smoke from the fire, and little dancing lights on the water. Suddenly Richard said, "Let's get over to the other side."

"What, swim?" Francis said hopefully.

"We could make a raft," he said.

"Golly! Yes. There's tons of wood up there," Francis exclaimed. "Do let's make a raft."

"Wouldn't we need rope or nails or something?" Penny said, then Richard lifted his rucksack on to his knees and began to undo the straps.

"I've got reams of rope," he said, "and all the necessary tools."

Tons of stuff seemed to come out of that rucksack; first his mackintosh rolled up, then a towel and some bathing clothes and a few extra jerseys. After that, a great coil of rope, and a little saw, and a wooden mallet, and an axe.

"I say—Richard!" Penny said excitedly. "Had you planned it all beforehand?"

"Where's all this wood you've been talking about?" he said, grinning, but we guessed he had planned it, all the same.

We didn't touch the stacks of wood or any of the really good-looking stuff, but there didn't seem any harm in using some of the smaller bits, and after a time we had selected and sawn up nine good logs for the job. Richard directed operations, but he made us all do our share of the work.

First we had to make some pegs with sharpened

ends, "pickets" he called them, and hammer them into the ground on either side of the logs to stop them rolling away. He made us put the smaller logs on the outside, "To make the raft more navigable."

Then we had to lash them all together at both ends, using figure-of-eight lashing, and this took a bit of doing and made us all frightfully hot and our hands rather sore. But we managed it all right.

"Golly!" Francis said. "What a job! D'you think it'll float?"

"Of course it will," Richard said, "but I think we ought to lash a spar or two at right angles first. It'll make the whole thing a bit more rigid."

"*You* can do that," Francis said. "I've got thousands of blisters all over my hands already."

But he helped all the same, and at last it was finished. We hammered out the pickets, and between us pushed our new raft down to the water's edge.

Richard made us all get into bathing shorts then, with the extra old jerseys he had brought with him on top.

"We'll probably get a bit wet," he said, "so we'd better keep our own clothes dry to go home in. Now help me shove the thing out, and I'll test it first."

We launched it out into the water, and Richard waded with it for several yards then climbed up, and it actually floated and supported him at the same time. It was an awfully exciting moment.

Of course we all wanted to get up at once, and were frightfully impatient when Richard said he must "drop the plumb-line" first. Actually he used his Scout staff, and could touch the bottom all the way over except just under the bank on the other side.

"Full-fathom-five down here!" he called. "Can you swim, Jep, in case we capsize?"

"Yes," I said. "Just about."

"Well, here goes, then!" He punted himself back to us, and we all scrambled up, one on each side to keep it balanced.

It floated all right, but it did let in the water, and if you sat down you got soaked!

We went to and fro dozens of times, taking it in turns to punt, and we all fell in at least once, and Francis tipped the whole thing over on top of himself! It was glorious fun, and none of us noticed how low the sun had got, nor how the sky was clouding over, and when Richard told us it was high time to come out and dress, we were all a bit mad with him. At least we were until we looked at the compass and found that it was after six o'clock!

"I've got a feeling it might be quicker to go on a bit, and come home by bus," Richard said. "It wasn't my original idea, but we seem to have left it a bit late. The main road can't be far off."

He stuffed all the wet things into his rucksack, then glanced round at us critically.

"You look blue, Jep," he said. "Have a race or something with Francis to get warm."

Then he and Penny went up through the wood to look for landmarks, and it was soon after this that Francis and I discovered the rapids. Of course they weren't real rapids, but the river-bed did go down rather suddenly, making a series of little waterfalls which splashed and gurgled over the stones in the most inviting way. Francis stood quite still, staring, then he said, in almost exactly Fin's voice:

"The thunder of the water and the feel of the spray in your face, it kinda goes to your head like wine!" And he turned his head suddenly and looked at me. "Come on, Jep. Let's shoot the rapids on the raft—quickly before Richard comes back."

We raced back along the bank for the raft, and, puffing like grampuses and laughing weakly, we heaved it along to the top of the "rapids". Then we climbed on and pushed off. It didn't go awfully well at first, because the rocks and things got in the way and we kept on getting stuck. But we managed to push ourselves free each time, and bumped and bounced and waltzed from one little waterfall to the next, shouting with joy, until suddenly we found ourselves in a swifter, deeper bit of the river which just took hold of the raft and slewed the whole thing over. I'm not quite sure what really happened then, except that I parted company with the raft and Francis, and got mouthfuls of river water and a terrific bang on the head from something jolly hard. It made me quite sick for a moment, then the next thing I remember clearly was scrambling on to a bit of flat rock, only to find that Francis was scrambling up it too from the other side.

"Oh! Jep," he spluttered, half laughing and half scared. "We were jolly nearly a couple of dead men then!"

"Where's the raft gone to?" I gasped. "We mustn't let it go."

"It's over there—stuck on something. We'd better try and rescue it."

But neither of us knew quite how, and we were trying to plan what to do when Richard and Penny came running along the river bank looking furious.

"If that's your idea of running a race, it isn't mine," Richard shouted out, and then he saw us on the rock in the river, and of course we were both drenched through.

"What the dickens——?" he began, then he stopped on the bank opposite to us and just stared.

"We were shooting the rapids, like Fin," Francis shouted, "and the raft capsized, but we're all right and the raft's over there."

"But Richard—they're absolutely soaked," Penny's voice sounded high against the running of the river and the rising wind, and I thought she looked a bit frightened.

"I know," Richard said grimly, then he jumped down among the rocks and stuck his staff into the water dividing us from the bank.

"It's O.K.," he said, "only a couple of feet deep. Come on, jump." And he held out his staff for us to hold on to, and pulled us, one at a time, on to the bank.

"You are a couple of idiots," he said, not really angry, but sort of fed up. "Why on earth did you have to try that game in your dry clothes? Just look at you!"

"What can we do?" Penny said dismally.

"I'm not going on the bus like this anyway,"

Francis said, "can't you light a fire and dry us, or something?"

"No I can't," Richard said, "it would take all night. There's only one thing—we'll have to walk it."

"But Richard, we won't be back till it's dark," Penny moaned.

"That isn't my fault. Come on you two—you'd better get going. It'll keep you warm." He looked at me suspiciously, "Feeling all right, Jep?"

"Only wet!" I said with a grin, deciding not to bother him with the lump on my head.

He made us leave the raft where it was, not too happily because after all it had been his idea, and we set off in a rather dismal little procession, the water squelching in our shoes at every step, and making walking beastly. Presently it began to rain.

"Get your mac on," Richard said to Penny. "The others might as well not bother."

"I didn't bring it," she said dolefully.

"Then have mine. Go on, and don't argue."

It was the longest walk I can ever remember, and all the way back sharp, scuddy showers of rain kept adding to our discomfort and making the air much colder.

"April showers!" was the last thing I can remember hearing Francis say before he shut up altogether, and by the time we reached The Well Cabin on our way to the village even Richard had given up trying to keep the conversation going. It was quite dark now, and I think Penny was almost crying with tiredness. Twice during the last mile Francis had tripped up on nothing and fallen flat in the mud, and my head felt as if it was going to burst open with the pain inside it.

"I think you'd all better go in to Fin," Richard said suddenly. "I'll go on and tell them at home."

We staggered gratefully up to the door, and Richard knocked on it with his Scout staff. Fin came out looking a bit mazed like he does when he's been writing a lot, but he soon came to when he saw it was us.

"We went a bit too far," Richard explained, "and these two asses fell into the river. D'you mind if they come in for a bit?"

"It looks as if they'd better," Fin said. "Did you ever see anything nearer to a batch of drowned rats?"

So we came in, dripping all over the hall, and Richard went on alone to break the news.

I was tugging at my sodden shoelaces, Francis sitting on the floor doing the same, and Penny struggling out of Richard's mackintosh, when the shivering attack began. It comes all of a sudden like that, and you can't do anything about it: it's just an awful helpless feeling.

"Oh Fin, what's happening to Jep?" I heard Penny's voice, then a second later Fin's too, quite near to me.

"What's up, Jep? Got chilled or something?"

"I—I c-c-can't h-help it——" I stuttered. "It's m-my t-t-tropical——"

"O.K. Don't try and talk," he said, and anyway it wasn't any good trying with my teeth chattering together like that. I should think both the others could hear the row they were making, and I couldn't even stand up straight.

I felt Fin's arm round me, and he carried me in by the fire and wrapped me up in a blanket.

"Here, drink this," he said, holding something to my lips.

"W-what is it? W-will it make me s-sick?"

"No. It'll stop you shaking. Come on."

I gulped it down, brandy or something, and it did seem to stop the shivering. But then I got to the burning stage. It's always the same; first the shivers, then the burning, then a frightful sweat which makes you shiver all over again.

"I don't think I could walk back to Blue Gates," I said muzzily.

"You don't have to," Fin said. "Just lie still, and go to sleep if you feel like it. There's nothing to worry about."

If I moved my head a bit I could see Francis and Penny sitting on the hearth-rug, Francis in some enormous garment of Fin's, and Penny in her own clothes but with bare feet. They were quite silent and eyeing me in a queer sort of way, but I felt too bad to worry.

Later a lot of people seemed to be talking all round me in loud voices, and I got carried off somewhere and put to bed. I can remember Fin's face, and Uncle Clive's too, I think, and Henrietta's cool hands doing things for me. But the whole thing was a bit of a nightmare, and all the time something kept beating away in my head.

I can remember saying weakly, "Where's it coming from? Is it the Red Indian drums?"

And Fin replying, "I guess it is, Jep; far away in the forests. It's the signal for getting off to sleep."

After that I think I must have gone to sleep.

CHAPTER THIRTEEN

SEBASTIAN AND A SHOCK

IT isn't much fun even to think about being ill, especially when you've got a bit of concussion as well as fever, so I'm not going to bother anyone with details. Anyhow I can't remember much about the next few days, except that I stayed in Fin's cabin and Henrietta was there looking after me. That was the best part, because she's jolly good at looking after people.

Then one morning I seemed to wake up properly, and the pain in my head had gone. There was a pale light showing behind the green curtains, and an absolute concert of bird song outside.

If you've ever been near a wood in April at dawn, you'll know what I mean; it's the most wonderful sound in the world. With a sigh of contentment I turned over on to my side, and then I saw Henrietta sitting in a chair by the fire and looking at me.

"Hullo!" I said, and we both smiled. "What time is it?"

"About half-past four. The sun will soon be up."

"Gosh! Is that all? Can you hear the dawn chorus?"

"Yes. Isn't it lovely? I hoped you would wake up and hear it too."

"Is Fin awake?"

"Yes. He's gone out, I think."

"Please can you draw the curtains?" I said. "I'd like to watch the sun rising."

Henrietta got up rather stiffly, and I wondered if she had been sitting there all night. She drew back the curtains and stood looking out into the early morning. I could see the dawn light shining on to her face, and I can remember thinking what a lovely face it was.

Presently the sun began to come up, very pale at first like a primrose petal, then growing brighter and brighter till suddenly it flooded the whole room with gold. I heard Fin come back to the house, then up the stairs and into my room almost without a sound, in case I was still asleep, I suppose. He was wearing his fringed Indian buckskin jacket which is what I like him in best, and he was holding a bunch of wild spring flowers still wet from the morning dew. He glanced at Henrietta, then at me.

"So you've decided it's time to get well, have you?" he said with a smile.

"Yes, Fin. Have I wasted an awful lot of time?"

"Not at all." He sat down by my bed. "Your blackcap was singing. Did you hear him?"

"Yes. Wasn't it a terrific dawn chorus? I suppose it's always like that here."

"I guess so, in the spring anyway."

He held out the flowers. "For you, Henrietta, for being such a good nurse to my boy."

We talked for a bit, the three of us together, then Henrietta gave me something to drink and I went off to sleep again.

Richard and Penny and Francis came to visit me the next day, one at a time.

"We got the raft back all right," Richard said, coming in first, "and we've put it safely away till the summer."

"Was it all right?"

"Yes, no damage at all. Fin says he'll help us to make a real canoe so that we can shoot the rapids properly. That old raft was far too big and clumsy."

"Yes, it was!" I said with a grin.

Penny hadn't got much to say for herself, and she looked a bit worried, I thought, as if something was on her mind, and she didn't seem sorry when her time was up and it was Francis's turn to come in.

He stood just inside the door with one hand in a bulging pocket, looking at me critically. Then he said, "You don't *look* any different!"

"Why should I?" I said.

"Well you ought to, after your tropical disease or whatever it was. I thought you'd look black or yellow or something!" Then he came over to my bed and lowered his voice. "I've got something for you, Jep. The others don't know yet."

He took a box out of his pocket and opened the lid. Up popped a small, short head with brilliant eyes.

"A slow-worm! I say, thanks awfully, Francis," I said.

"I don't know where you're going to keep him," he said. "This box is a bit too small I'm afraid. He's called Sebastian, by the way."

I lifted Sebastian carefully out of the box, and for a moment he stayed quite still on my hand, just like a piece of solid bronze, and quite smooth all over.

Then suddenly he got frightened, and slipped through my fingers over the edge of the bed on to the floor. Francis dived after him and upset the table with my medicine on it. There was a terrific crash which brought Fin up the stairs to see what was happening.

"It's Sebastian," Francis explained, poking a red face out from under my bed. "He escaped, but I've caught him again. He's frightfully energetic."

"Where can I keep him, Fin?" I asked.

"He prefers to spend most of his time under a flat stone or in a burrow, then he comes out at dusk to feed. I guess we'd better find a suitable lodging for him in the garden, and just hope he stays."

"When can Jep get up again?" Francis asked.

"That depends on your dad, and Jep himself. Now come on, Francis, help me clear up this terrible mess you've made, then we'll get Sebastian settled outside."

I made up my mind to get better jolly quickly, and I was doing fine until Penny told me what was on her mind, and then everything seemed to go wrong for a bit.

It was Good Friday, and she must have come straight over to The Cabin after church, for she arrived very out of breath and came panting up the stairs to my room.

"They don't know I'm here, Jep, but I simply couldn't settle down to picking flowers till I'd told you."

I can still see her now if I shut my eyes and think, standing in the middle of the floor with sunlight shining on to her copper-coloured hair and making it look quite golden, and she was wearing a blue jumper and a grey skirt; I can remember every detail clearly, because it was one of the worst moments of my life.

"Told me what?" I said.

"About—Aunt June."

"What about her? Has something happened to her?" I had seen her only the evening before, and she seemed all right then.

"Nothing's happened to her exactly," Penny said, "but she talks to herself, and the other day when you were so bad, I heard her saying over and over again to herself, 'It will be quite impossible for me to keep him if he's delicate.' It was awful, Jep, and I've been terribly worried ever since; I haven't said anything to anyone else, but I thought you ought to know."

She gave me rather a pathetic look, then went off to pick flowers for Easter with the rest of the family.

Well, this seemed like the end as far as I was concerned, and when Fin came up to say that Sebastian was still there, he found me crying myself blind! I couldn't help it.

Of course he was awfully decent, and asked if my head was bad, or if anything was wrong, and if he could help at all, but I said "No" to everything for somehow I just could not tell him the truth. But I couldn't eat any dinner or tea, and by the evening my head was aching again. I can remember thinking vaguely that if I died she couldn't send me away, but it wasn't a very helpful thought!

I slept badly and had horrid dreams that night,

and in the morning I didn't care when Fin told me that the house-martins had arrived.

"Two pairs," he said, "and it looks as if they're thinking about nesting under the eaves of this cabin. I've never had that honour before."

"Haven't you," I said dimly.

"And I think, but I'm not sure, that the long-tailed tits have built in the hedge opposite," he went on. "I daren't disturb them yet to make sure, but we'll find out soon."

I hadn't got any answer to that one, because what was the use of a long-tailed tit's nest if I wasn't going to be there to watch it?

Uncle Clive turned up in the afternoon—I suppose they sent for him because I wouldn't eat, and I had made up my mind to tell him that I was feeling much worse again.

But he didn't ask me how I was feeling this time.

"What's all this?" he said instead, looking at me very straight.

"I feel worse," I said.

"Of course you do with an empty stomach, anybody would."

"I *can't* eat," I said miserably.

Uncle Clive pulled a chair up to the bed and sat down. "Look here, Jep," he said. "You're not going to help anyone by going on a hunger strike, least of all yourself. What's the big idea?"

"I'm worse again," I mumbled.

He smiled then, kindly, but in a way which made me feel a bit silly. "Come on, what's worrying you? You might as well tell me."

"Nothing. I just feel awful," I said.

"Do you think Henrietta's cooking's going to poison you or something?"

"Of course not," I said, and I couldn't help smiling a bit because it was such a daft idea!

"Well, she'll be glad to know that, anyway. She was getting quite worried."

I knew he was only pulling my leg now, and it suddenly seemed a bit cracked not to tell him the real reason.

"It's Aunt June," I said, all of a sudden.

"What; does she poison you then?"

"No," I laughed weakly. "It's what she said—Penny told me."

He waited for me to go on.

"She said she heard her saying over and over again that she couldn't possibly keep me if I was delicate."

"Who said you were delicate?" Uncle Clive said. "It's the first I've heard of it."

"It's my tropical fever—everyone gets a panic when I get it, then they send me away—it isn't fair, and I don't want to go away again."

Uncle Clive crossed one leg over the other, and bent forward, looking hard into my face.

"Look here, Jep," he said. "I want you to get all silly ideas about this tropical fever business right out of your head. You may have had it once when you lived abroad, but that's all dead and done with years ago. You got properly chilled on Sunday, that's all, and a good old bang on the head into the bargain! I think you're as tough as nails."

"But they always said it was tropical fever because I was born in Nigeria."

"Then they just got it wrong," Uncle Clive said with a smile.

"You'll tell Aunt June, won't you?" I said after a bit.

"Yes, I'll tell her. Now, what about some tea? Hungry yet?"

"Yes, I think I am a bit," I said. "Now that I know. It was awfully worrying, Uncle Clive. I *don't* want to have to go away any more, you know."

"You won't have to, Jep," he said.

When Fin came up with my tea, I felt a bit silly till he called me a "Koko-koho", which is Red Indian for an Owl! Then Henrietta came rushing up too to say that she had forgotten to put the arsenic in my tea, and we all laughed like anything; it was such a colossal relief.

The sun simply blazed out on Easter Morning, and Fin pushed my bed up to the window so that I could sit and bask in it, and hear the church bells ringing out across the fields, and smell the blossom and the freshness of the woods.

CHAPTER FOURTEEN

"COME AND LIVE WITH US"

I WAS allowed to have a big bit of the summer term as an extra holiday to get quite better in, and although I was back again at Blue Gates then, I spent more than half my time with Fin. I think that that May and June were even more glorious than the April before them, with the sun shining down from the blue sky, you just felt bursting with happiness!

After one long day together, Fin and I went up on to Raywhistle Brow in the evening and sat looking down over the valley. The hum of tractor engines drifted up to us on the warm summer air smelling faintly of new mown hay, and we could see the figures of the farm workers below us moving to and fro like busy ants. Fin had been quiet for a long time, even longer than he sometimes is, but I didn't mind as long as we were together.

Then suddenly he said, "Jep, I want to ask you something."

"What?" I said, lying on my front with my chin propped up in my hands.

"Do you mind if I marry Henrietta?"

I rolled on to my side and looked up at him.

"Does Henrietta mind?" I asked.

"No, not if you don't. As a matter of fact she's quite keen on the idea."

"Then I don't mind either. I think it's an awfully good thing, really."

"I'm glad you agree," he said. "And that starts up another little matter to be settled too."

"What about?"

"About you this time. We'd rather like you to come along and live with us at The Well Cabin, if you'd care to?"

Well, I simply couldn't say anything for a moment; it just didn't seem possible; but when I saw that he really did mean it, I said:

"It's the most marvellous, wonderful, glorious thing that's absolutely ever happened!"

Fin laughed then, and he sounded awfully happy.

"That's settled, then. We didn't somehow think you'd object."

"Does Aunt June know?"

"Nobody knows yet. We wanted you to be the first."

"Then don't you think we'd better tell her," I said, getting up from the grass. I didn't want to waste a single minute.

"What's the great hurry, Jep?" Fin said lazily. "I guess she won't raise any objections, not when we explain things."

"But I want her to know now," I said. "I want to make quite sure she won't mind. After all, she's been jolly decent to me."

"O.K. then," he said, heaving himself on to his feet. "Let's go and rout out Henrietta, then spill the beans around. They'll all have to know sooner or later."

We found Aunt June picking roses in her garden

at Blue Gates. She looked up at the click of the gate.

"Dear me, this looks quite like a deputation," she said as we came up the path. "I wonder what can have brought you all together like this?"

"Something awfully important, Aunt June," I said. "Fin and Henrietta are going to get married, and they want me to go and live with them for always at The Well Cabin. Do you mind?"

She didn't say anything for a moment, but just stood and looked at us with the roses in her hand. I thought she was going to cry or something, but then Aunt June's like that when things are rather special. After an awfully anxious moment for me, she said:

"But who am I to mind, Jeffrey, when a real mother and father have come along for you at last? Dear me, this is very exciting news indeed. I really don't know who to congratulate first."

Henrietta made it easy for her by going up and giving her a kiss, then Fin did the same, so of course I had to too and this seemed to please her a lot. Dear Aunt June; she's awfully sweet, but I couldn't have lived with her for ever. I see that now.

On the evening before the wedding I slipped away alone to The Well Cabin. I ought to have been in bed, really, but everyone was so busy getting things ready for the next day that I didn't think they would miss me. I found Fin leaning on the new garden gate and quietly smoking his pipe.

"Hullo! Jep," he said. "Escaped for a bit of peace, like me?"

"Rather!" I said. "There's a frightful fuss going on back there."

He opened the gate to let me into the garden, and as I went through it something moved in the grass at our feet. We both peered downwards.

"Sebastian," Fin said. "He's still with us, you see."

It was nearly dark now except for a faint pinkness in the north-west sky, and the flowering ramblers over the porch showed up very white. The warm air was quite heavy with the scent of roses and honeysuckle, then suddenly a nightingale began to sing from the wood, its lovely song throbbing out into the stillness.

We listened for a bit without talking, then Fin laid a big hand on my shoulder and said confidently, "The beginning of a new life for all of us, Jep."

"Yes." I looked up at him. "And it's going to be absolutely my last new beginning for ever and ever, isn't it, Fin?"

"I guess it is," he said, looking down at me, and although it was almost dark I could see that he was smiling like anything.